POLAND

POLAND

Jill Stephenson
and
Alfred Bloch

HIPPOCRENE BOOKS, INC.
New York

Hippocrene revised edition, 1993.

For information, address:
Hippocrene Books, Inc.
171 Madison Avenue
New York, NY 10016

Library of Congress Cataloging-in-Publication Data
Stephenson, Jill.
        Hippocrene companion guide to Poland/Jill Stephenson and Alfred
Bloch.
        ISBN 0-87052-636-7
        1. Poland—Description and travel—1981- —Guide-books.
I. Bloch, Alfred, 1922- . II. Title.
DK4037.S74 1990
90-19527
914.3804'56—dc20   CIP

ISBN 0-7818-0077-3 (revised edition)

Printed in the United States of America.

CONTENTS

Introduction   7

Almanac for Travelers   11

Poland of the 90s and the Tourist   15

1. The Unique Culture of Poland   21

2. Warsaw: The Story Told by the Old Town
   Market   27

3. Warsaw: The Story Told by the Royal Castle   33

4. Warsaw: The Story Told by Three Monuments   39

5. Warsaw: The Story Told by the Church of the
   Holy Cross and Chopin's Heart   47

6. Warsaw: The City and How to Enjoy All It
   Has to Offer   53

7. A Respite from the Twentieth Century   61

8. Krakow: The City of Kings, Prelates and
   Learning   71

9. The Mountains, the Forests and Their Fiercely
   Independent People   83

10. Along the Mountain Range to the Core of the
    Peasant Country   89

11. Gniezno: The Cradle of Polish Catholicism   99
12. Gdansk and the Beauty of the Baltic Sea   107
13. The Pleasures of the Unexpected   115
14. The Cradle of Art   123
15. A Cradle for Artists   131
16. The Tale of Two Cities: Poznan and Wroclaw   137
17. The "Inner" Culture   145
18. Sporting Life   157
19. Epilogue   169
Appendix: Reflections on the Capital of "New
    Freedom"   173
Index   177

Introduction to Revised Edition

Freedom is indeed a heady wine. If the noble product of the grape is kept corked up for centuries as it was in the case of the Russian/Soviet Empire or in Poland where it remained in the barrel for half a century, the contents explode. The force of the explosion propels the sediment at the bottom of the barrel to the top and obscures the clarity and real taste of the wine.

Translated into social terms, there is a lot of sediment—immoral, dishonest, conniving social elements—which are the first to benefit from the new-found freedom. They reach the top, they cause confusion within the country, and they are responsible for the hesitancy of older established democracies to associate too closely with Poland.

The truth of that phenomenon has been evident to the new political leadership of Poland, and slowly but perceptibly the "sediment" is being relegated to the place it deserves. The energetic forces emerging in leadership positions—in the political and economic spheres—are creating the structures, climate and real confidence building procedures which will create a market economy and a responsible government.

The power of the sediment is real and the struggle against it has not yet been won. The sediment is not composed of simply the old *nomenclatura* of the Polish Communist Regime. Some of the managers of that regime, some of the companies and industries created by that regime, are vital, capably managed, and very useful. But many of the nomenclatura allied themselves with the wheelers and dealers that always flourished in Poland which strengthened them by allowing them to maintain illicit foreign bank accounts thus enabling them to emerge on the international markets as well-financed traders. In fact these traders flourish by smuggling, selling shoddy goods, cheating and stealing. But, they could not flourish if they did not find willing partners in all the areas formerly identified as the "free world."

This economic phenomenon has its strictly social counterpart. Not confined to ostentatious consumption evidenced by the number of Mercedes, Porches, BMWs and expensive boutiques bought by this parody of an economic elite, it is also unpleasantly visible in the increase in street crimes, petty thievery, and a general visible void of normal social intercourse. Poland is a country in turmoil, but it is a fascinating turmoil.

For a tourist and even for a serious businessman, a trip to Poland today is a voyage to the roots of our own economic history—filled with vision, imagination, sculduggery, corruption, and the eventual elevation of success. It was never easy to mix capitalism with democracy. It was never simple to join competition, free market economies and the race to excel with the ethical demands of real democracy. It took the U.S. centuries, a bloody civil war, a shameful Indian policy, and legalized discrimination against black Americans which we only recently began to dismantle, before democracy (imperfect that it still is) and capitalism could find an accommodation that would serve the needs of both. Fortunately we had a continent in which this still far from perfect fusion could occur. Poland never had this luxury. The people of Poland had to fight so many wars, live through so many occupations that they never had time to learn the workings of a democratic system or gain the experiences of a capitalist economy.

What they are achieving in two years of freedom, what they are accomplishing largely with their own resources, is worthy of a world audience. But like all Poland's great achievements, this one too finds little echo in either the mass media in the U.S. or in the formulation of international economic policies. Again, Poland is discarded because of a morbid fascination with Russia, even though it was the people of Poland, it was the success of Solidarity that shocked the "evil empire" into the state of collapse. Are the Polish people destined today to receive the same rewards they received for being the first to say "NO" to Hitler?

If there ever was a time to visit Poland, it is now. The sense of exuberance has to be felt, the struggles have to be seen, and a lot of real fun can be had while viewing democracy and capitalism acting together to create a splendid scene. Being a spectator or an actor in the unfolding of the historical epic on a magnificent stage is an experience that people should not deny themselves.

Almanac for Travelers

Due to the fundamental political and economic changes taking place in Republic of Poland, nearly all the information contained in this special section relevant to prices and export/import regulations is subject to change. We urge you to check the information with either the Cultural Attache, Polish Embassy, 2640 16th Street, N.W., Washington, DC 20009 (202/234-3800) or the Cultural Attache, Polish Consulate General, 233 Madison Avenue, New York, NY 10016, (212/889-8216). We recommend that you inquire by phone or letter specifically about the latest regulations concerning imports and exports of merchandise to and from Poland, especially if you plan to take any gifts into the country or make any purchases while there.

The other source of reliable information is the tourist office ORBIS, 342 Madison Avenue, Suite 1512, New York, NY 10173, (212/867-5011). The telephones are usually busy, so we suggest you write to them. ORBIS can give you current hotel prices, send you brochures and suggest itineraries.

The only direct flights to Poland are offered by the Polish airline LOT, which now operates a Boeing 767 and offers business and tourist class accommodations. The comfort and service of LOT are superb, so is the food. The flights leave from JFK at about 4 PM and arrive at Warsaw's Okecie Airport at 7 AM. The actual flying time is about eight and one-half hours. In our experience the departures and arrivals were on time.

The tickets vary in price from as little as $700 for a round trip to as much as $1,200 for a one-way business class ticket. You should purchase your tickets through a reputable travel agency. Usually they can get you the best prices. LOT is a very popular airline and we suggest that you get to JFK a good two hours prior to departure. Poles carry enormous amounts of luggage and if you come late you may find yourself standing in long lines to check-in.

You can reach Poland by flying on major European airlines. If you use any of these lines you will have to change planes at their principal European destination. This usually requires a one-hour wait and a change of planes to a smaller twin engine one.

When President Walesa visited the United States he promised that Poland will have an open border. He kept his word; there are no visa requirements. All you need is a valid passport and you must have hotel reservations. The only hotels you should go to are those that have four stars or at least three. These hotels are heavily booked because Warsaw has become an international center for trade and finance, and, without reservations, you might find yourself shunted to a third-rate hotel, which is not a pleasant experience! The only other thing you need is money. If you want to buy antiques—which are a good buy now—works of art, tailor-made suits, etc., you can still find wonderful bargains.

Poland is not for tourists who have to travel on a restricted budget. Unless you are young, willing to use buses to travel from one location to another, or hitchhike and live on camping grounds, a vacation in Poland is as expensive as it is in any other Western European country, except that, as yet, there are no charming inexpensive inns, or clean hotels for the tourist on a short budget.

Take with you what you would take if you went to visit Italy, Austria, or Switzerland. You will find everything you need in contemporary Poland.

The Polish monetary unit is the zloty. Since the assumption of power by the freely elected government dedicated to the introduction of a capitalist system, the zloty is freely convertible into dollars, or any hard currency, at the prevailing market rate. Conversely the dollar is also freely convertible into zlotys. There are official currency exchange agencies at the airport and in cities. The current rate of exchange is approximately 11,500 zlotys to the dollar. You will be expected to pay for your hotel accommodations in dollars, but meals and everything else you buy in Poland can be paid for in zlotys. If you have zlotys left over when you are ready to leave, you can purchase dollars with them at the agencies or hotels.

We should add to this list one recommendation that Americans usually resist: You should learn a little Polish before you take your trip. If you happen to live in the State of New York, you can take "a total immersion course" in Polish at the State University College at New Paltz. If that is inconvenient, you can buy Polish language tapes at Berlitz or the leading bookstore in your town. A knowledge of Polish will magnify beyond calculation the pleasure of your visit. For those visitors who intend to go to Poland for an extended stay, perhaps to study or to take advantage of the many opportunities open to painters, sculptors, film makers, and photographers, or who may wish to do business in the burgeoning free market hungry for all manner of goods, we strongly recommend the six-weeks course offered by the Jagiellonian University of Krakow. You will not only learn the language, but become acquainted with Poland's superb literature and its always fascinating history. You will also acquire many friends and enjoy a rich social life. You can make all the necessary arrangements through the Cultural Attache or directly with the University by writing to the Director of the Language Program for Foreigners. You do not have to have a university degree to participate in this program. The course, including living accommodations in dormitories, is quite inexpensive. Prices are subject to change, but the cost should not exceed $1,000. While there in Krakow, you will be close to the most picturesque region of Poland.

Poland of the 90s and the Tourist

There is no "free market economy" anywhere in the industrialized world. All economies are subsidized, all governments
provide protection for some segments of their industry. Most
economies are "managed" either by the manner in which the
government allocates its budget or by powerful families. The
Polish government, however, decided on "shock therapy" for
its transition from communism to capitalism. As a result of
this traditional cavalry-charge mentality they destroyed the
entire economic network built up during forty years of communist rule, and replaced it with "chaos."

The idea for the "shock treatment" actually was Harvard-
bred and MBA blessed, but it appealed to the Polish mentality
magnificently captured by a Polish proverb *"Motyka na
slonce,"* which conveys the notion of going on a wild goose
chase.

The existence of a direct relationship between democracy

and a "free market economy" is still debatable, but the acceptance of this relationship by the current Polish government
has consequences both for tourists and businessmen to
whom this version of the book is dedicated.

For the tourist who is not familiar with Poland and has no
friends in Poland, Warsaw and the other interesting cities as
well have become among the most expensive cities in Europe.
A room in a Marriott Hotel, which in an American city like
Washington, D.C., would be $175 at most per night, is $205
at the Warsaw Marriott. The Holiday Inn, which advertises
on U.S. television rooms well below $100 per night, charges
about $165 plus in Poland. While there are many good restau-
rants in Poland, the menus are unimaginative. The main
dishes are either veal, beef, or, the most popular, pork. A
meal in a Polish restaurant need not cost more than $20—
that is if you do not have a glass of wine with the meal. This
"luxury" will more than double your tab.

The Poles who can afford it will not drink Polish milk, but
will go to a delicatessen and buy German, Dutch, or Danish
milk products and eggs—not because they are better, but because they are cheaper. (In the case of Polish milk, however,
the milk is frequently contaminated, and the bottles are not
properly cleaned.) This is due to policies of the government
and to the obstinacy of the Polish peasant. Western democracies understand the concept of subsidy and therefore the
Dutch farmer can sell an egg very cheaply, while the government guarantees against losses. In Poland, the Communist
government bought everything the peasants produced at
stated prices. Then, due to the government inefficiency, half
of what it bought was lost on the way to the marketplace. But
the peasant was paid and the fertilizers, equipment, etc.,
were made available at subsidized prices, including diesel
fuel and gasoline.

The new Polish government cut out the subsidies and
stopped the purchase guarantees. The peasant is on his own.
He, the Polish worker—the Polish manager, the Polish artists,
writers, painters—are for the first time in half a century on
their own, abruptly left to their own devices. The prevailing

motto is "do the best you can." Honest, hard-working, dedicated people rarely come out on top during the first phases of existence in an economic jungle. The winners are the manipulators, con men, etc. But that is not the fault of either the government or the International Monetary Fund, or the World Bank—their errors are much graver and still have long lasting ill effects.

The conditions prevailing in Poland arise from the fact that not even a wealthy government could afford to subsidize the highly inefficient farm industry. There are about 10 million farms in Poland accounting for about one-third of Poland's population. No government can afford to subsidize one-third of its population.

The basic problem of democracy and free markets is the way they are perceived. The Poles—except for the handful of specialists—do not understand how that new system works. Every tourist, every business person traveling to Poland can help build an understanding of a system which holds many mysteries, harbors nuances, and responds to obscure stimuli like consumer confidence. Everyone visiting Poland now is in a very special way a teacher, while simultaneously being a student of a growing social reality.

Usually the "pampered" Western tourist does not want to be challenged, does not want to participate in the society he or she may visit. The magic key is in the word "participation." In Poland the concept of participation has deep historical roots, because Poland was a gentry democracy before America was even discovered. The Polish people were seldom spectators of historical events—they were usually the principal actors of tragic fate. In recent centuries whenever they actively participated, they lost. They lost so often that now, when their participation is desperately needed, they do not know how to engage. Given a chance at free elections the Poles elected representatives from 29 diverse political parties. The government can never be sure that it can muster a majority of votes for the most basic programs. The president could rule by decree but that would be for the Poles a sort of return to Stalinism. You, as the visitor, may not know too well what participation means either, but you can illustrate how differences of opinion can be channeled into a system without causing traumas. You can debate issues without becoming angry at those who support different ones. You can talk about town meetings, precinct meetings, the concept of civilian control and the deeply ingrained devotion to the Bill of Rights. And if that is not your "cup of tea," you can explain how to build up a small business, how to create day care centers without government funds, how to sustain a theater by voluntarism. In short, you can be an ambassador, not of an imperial power, but an ambassador of your way of thinking, your way of doing the myriads of small things that make a system work.

Danger always accompanies radical changes. In our first edition of this book we told you about the safety of Polish streets even at night. That is no longer true. Poland's imports from the West were not only capitalism and democracy but also AIDS, drugs, street crime, violence, rape and murder. During the day you have to look out for pickpockets (as in Rome and Paris, for example), and at night, if you do venture out of your hotel, use a taxi, go in groups, and stay in the good section of town.

In Poland's major cities, it is fun just walking the well lit streets to see the attractive shop window displays and visit art galleries in which the artist is no longer "approved by the regime" and can produce art freely. Even the street vendors are colorful characters and, yes, when you are ready to take a break from your sightseeing, you can even get a good pizza. There are good things in the "free market economy" for the Polish people and the Polish tourist in the 90s.

CHAPTER ONE

The Unique Culture of Poland

The culture of any society develops over centuries into a colorful mosaic integrated into an appealing unity by the effect of dominant pieces. In Italy it is the grandeur of the Roman Empire, the splendor of the Catholic Church, the proud audacity of Renaissance art and the calculated splendor of famous city states like Venice, Florence, Milan and dozens of others which contribute to its culture. In France it is the awesome splendor of Gothic cathedrals, the inimitable opulence of palaces crowned by the ultimate expression of royal dynastic absolutism—Versailles—matched only by the Arch of Triumph, the symbolic expression of the French Revolution and the Napoleonic dream of hegemony over the European continent. The universally known Eiffel Tower is the lasting emblem of the predominance of Paris as the intellectual and industrial center of the old continent.

Other European societies evolved cultures based on an unbridled love of commerce, tangible wealth, and empire building, the prime examples being Holland, Spain and England. However, it is Germany, due to her geographic location at the center of Europe, that stamped the character, structure and content identified as "European culture." Although politically Germany was a collection of more or less independent kingdoms, duchies and a variety of provinces, the country nevertheless always played a major role in shaping the history and culture of neighbors. One of the principal reasons for this pre-eminence of Germany is the fact that Otto I, crowned Emperor of Germany in 962, also received from Pope John XII the title of Holy Roman Emperor of the German Nation. This distinction, first held by Charlemagne who in the year 800 declared himself to be the successor of the Roman Empire, acquired a different meaning in 962. The institution of the Holy Roman Emperor indicated that the Pope was the spiritual Vicar of Christ, while the Emperor claimed to be the temporal Vicar of Christ and thus the rule of Christendom in Europe. This largely theoretical sovereignty survived until 1806, when Francis II, Emperor of Austria, having been defeated by Napoleon, gave up the title.

Institutions like the Holy Roman Empire may have limited political power; they do exert enormous influences on the formation and content of cultures. They also create an aura of dependency. Christianity came to Poland from Germany in 966, and on the wave of this conversion, which was not completed until the 13th century, came German laws and customs which will be described in subsequent chapters. The real foundations of German influence in Europe were built by the proud, wealthy, independent burghers—the semantic and real root of what we call the bourgeoisie or the middle class.

The mosaic of Poland's culture is substantially different. Although the Catholic Church did play a role in shaping some of the major pieces of the mosaic, it was not the predominant theme. The territory we now identify as Poland was never part of the Roman Empire and never really shared nor was directly influenced by the fall out of Latin culture and the imperial social structure. Lying on the fringes of the Roman Empire and being far from the Byzantine Empire, Poland's people evolved their own independent way of being and seeing the world, and created its own life styles. In short, in the mosaic of Poland's culture there are only three major outstanding pieces: the love of land, the worship of individuality and freedom, and national pride.

Poland did not have feudal lords; it did not have an aristocracy similar to France's princes, dukes, marquis, counts and barons. Poland's aristocracy gained its distinction through service to the country.

At the pinnacle of Poland's social structure were the magnates, whose roots are one of the unsolved mysteries of history. They owned hundreds of thousands of acres of land, created towns and built magnificent palaces. The magnates were frequently wealthier than the kings. They were patrons of the arts. They imported the best of the Renaissance builders and painters to decorate their mansions and to design their cities. They invited scholars to bring education and refinement into the life styles of Poland's rich and famous.

The handful of magnates were economically supported, their life styles copied, and their manners imitated by a uniquely Polish social stratum, the *szlachta* (pronounced "shlakta"). The *szlachta* owned much less land, frequently not more than a few acres, built smaller but also pretentious homesteads, spent their time fighting, hunting, and made the joy of living the supreme goal of their lives. They questioned all authority, but accepted grudgingly life within the law. Yet they were also very curious, desirous of being educated, anxious to travel and searched for adventures of the mind and the sword.

Far below the *szlachta*, in terms of wealth, education, and desire for more than survival, were the peasants—the folk of Poland. The only characteristic they acquired from the *szlachta* was the desire to be left alone. For centuries Poland's peasants were free. They did not share the role of beasts of burden that was the fate of Western and Eastern European brethren. During the thousands of years of Poland's history, the peasants were subjugated for about three centuries, long enough to push them into abject poverty and imprison them in ignorance which imbued them with an intolerance that survived until late into the 20th century. Their solace was the Church; their humanity was expressed by simple, colorful folk art. Art was the only area open to their dreams and was accessible despite their ignorance. An illiterate peasant could produce wood sculptures, colorful paintings, intricate leather designs, and build simple yet magnificently decorated wooden churches.

This unique social structure produced two cultures within one mosaic: the culture of the magnates/*szlachta* and the culture of the peasants. To this date they have not merged and you will see the evidence of both while you travel through Poland.

The great cultural impact of Western Europe on Poland is visible in Poland's major cities. Cities like Warsaw, Krakow, Poznan and Gdansk were protected by royal decrees, while others were taken under royal protection because they were populated basically by German burghers, merchants and traders who, in turn, brought into existence a native Polish class of artisans. They learned their trade from German masters. Thus, while the cities created by the magnates will resemble Italian towns (Zamosc, for example) the old sections of Warsaw and Krakow will show a striking similarity to medieval German towns.

Added to the heady social mixture of native Poles are two ingredients which made Poland nigh well impossible to govern effectively. Poland, because of its union with the Grand Dutchy of Lithuania (1386–1569) with frontiers extended to the Baltic in the north and the outskirts of Moscow in the east, became a multi-national kingdom. Included in this mixture of people are 75 percent of all of Europe's Jews, who flocked into this multi-national kingdom (from the mid-14th century on) because it was tolerant and gave the Jews the legal right to be governed by their own laws, customs and elected officials.

The second special element in the mosaic of Poland's culture that was and remains unique is that since the late 16th century, Poland's kings were elected. Poland was the largest kingdom on the European continent and to be named king was a worthwhile prize. It is not surprising that Europe's voracious royal dynasties did all they could to get one of their own elected king of Poland. Elections took place in the vicinity of Warsaw. The electorate consisted of all members of the *szlachta*, the magnates and the clergy. According to the best available 18th-century estimates there were 800,000 Poles eligible to participate in the elections, a number equalled by the Western democracies only late in the 19th century. Thus Poland earned its reputation as a "gentry democracy."

With 800,000 electors and a number of very influential magnates, the candidates for the throne used every political device possible to defeat their rivals. The process resembled New York City ward politics even before the world dreamed that there would be a United States. Obviously, the candidates sought to outbid each other in promising what they would give to the *szlachta* and to the magnates in order to obtain their votes. Once one of them was elected, he had to deliver. The result was such a restricted royal power that very little could be accomplished. Poland slowly descended into anarchy. Only the magnates were sufficiently powerful to maintain a semblance of order in their provinces which they ruled in the manner of Chinese warlords.

Politics, good and bad, became the game Poles learned to love to play. These politics were usually the politics of opposition; Poles are truly magnificent and fearless in opposition. Unfortunately they have very little experience in transforming politics into policies. In short, Poland's politicians never learned the art of governing a people living in the modern world, for which they paid a very high price. (We shall have more to say on this subject later on in the book.) The point we want to make now is that to understand Poland's culture, you have to be very aware of Poland's political past. In Poland, there is a saying, "Everything is politics." In Poland that is true more so than in many other sovereign state.

Welcome to Poland, welcome to Warsaw.

CHAPTER TWO

Warsaw: The Story Told by the Old Town Market

As you stand in front of your hotel in Warsaw, close your eyes and stretch your mind to its very limit. Imagine a sea of tumbled gray ruins reaching to the horizon, most of them no higher than three feet. That was Warsaw forty-five years ago and in fact the image fits nearly all of Poland at the end of World War II. The very sights you are about to see and visit as a tourist are the collective expressions of Polish patriotism and love of country despite the bungling corruption and repression, characteristic of a system imposed on Poland by Stalin in

1948, planned by him as early as 1939, when the Soviet Union signed the non-aggression pact with Nazi Germany. This agreement was a prelude to the rape of a nation, but "rape" is really too weak a word to describe the crimes perpetrated by the two monsters for whom there is no adequate classification.

Warsaw was the graveyard of the Jewish martyrs who in April of 1943 ignited the Ghetto Uprising, chosing to die with arms in their hands rather than be led to slaughter in concentration camps.

Warsaw was the graveyard of Polish Freedom Fighters who on August 1, 1944, fought to liberate their capital by defeating the SS Troups who murdered them, degraded them and tried to reduce them to slaves of the Thousand Year Reich. The Freedom Fighters' defeat was cynically applauded by Stalin, who ordered the splendidly equipped Red Army to stop on the Eastern Bank of the Vistula, a fifteen or twenty minute walk from where you may be standing, and watch Warsaw burn. A Warsaw liberated by the Polish Patriotic Home Army would have led to the establishment of a victorious, independent, democratic Poland. It would have thus prevented the creation of Stalin's evil empire.

The Western Allies share the blame for both tragedies. They helped neither the Jews in their desperate fight to survive nor the Poles in the instant when glory and hope were within grasp. The awesome ruins of Warsaw were a monument to ineptness, extreme callousness, and deliberate demonic calculation. The ruins are no more, but the memory will never be erased. Their consequences are still visible in the politics of Poland, in the psyche of the people, and all along the tortuous road to recovery being traversed by 38 million Poles. Only now, forty-five years after the end of World War II, can the Poles act independently to restore their country to political, emotional and economic health. Forty-five years equals three generations.

Warsaw was partially destroyed in September 1939 and later so completely destroyed during the uprising which lasted from August 1, 1944, to the end of September of that year that there were plans to move the capital of Poland to

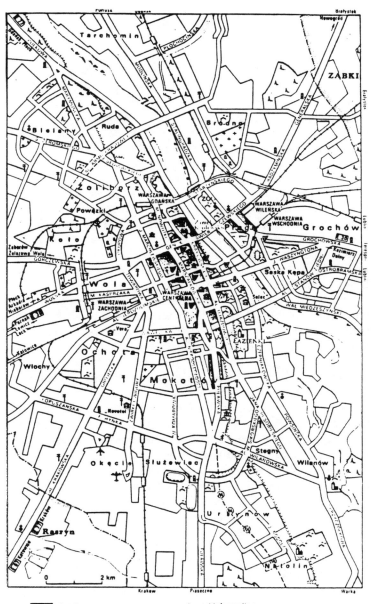

![Old Town] Old Town	![tourist information] tourist information
![information and shopping center] information and shopping center	![museums] museums
![railway stations] railway stations	![historical monuments] historical monuments
![subway] subway	![theaters] theaters
![ORBIS Incoming Foreign Tourism Office] ORBIS Incoming Foreign Tourism Office	![automobile service stations] automobile service stations
![ORBIS hotels] ORBIS hotels	![gasoline stations] gasoline stations (open 24 hr)

another site and build a new city similar to Brasilia, the created capital of Brazil. But that plan was never really seriously considered because all the Poles, not only the Warsovians, wanted a Warsaw as it was before Hitler's divebombers began their work of destruction. The Polish people chose to rebuild their city with the incomparable patience of restorers prompted by a visible devotion to their history. The reconstruction was an act of restoring the continuity of the Polish history the Nazis had tried to erase.

Although the first capital of Poland was Krakow, Warsaw became the capital at the whim of a hunt-loving Swedish prince who was elected king of Poland in 1587, and in 1596 moved the capital from Krakow to Warsaw. At that time Poland was the largest land power in Europe with frontiers extending from the Baltic Sea to the Black Sea, from the Oder River to Smolensk, and beyond Kiev.

Actually at the time it became the capital, Warsaw was a small town of 20,000 inhabitants whose livelihood was a brisk trade in wood and grain from the huge forests of Poland and the abundant stream of golden wheat and oat grains harvested from the black earth of the granary of Europe, a distinction accorded to the South Eastern provinces of the kingdom, now identified as the Ukraine.

The wooden masts of the famous English sailing ships of Sir Francis Drake and Lord Essex came from the tall pine trees still found in the Tatra Mountains of modern Poland—such ships were also stocked with provisions exported by Poland. But it was not the trading potential of Warsaw that enticed the king to move the capital; it was the abundance of game readily found in the dense forests that still surround Warsaw and which in more recent years were the favorite hiding places of Poles fighting for freedom.

You can stroll from your hotel to the old market square where it all began and in a walk of about one mile unravel the history of Poland in its original setting. (Well not quite original, but restored to the way it was, down to the most minute details.)

After the war, Polish craftsmen, artisans, painters, sculptors, iron workers, archivists and historians did their best to preserve for you and future generations of Poles a living, vibrant, fully functional market square. Its official name now is the Old Town Market located in Old Town. Except for presence of men and women of the 20th century, there are no intrusive signs of our times to dispell the 15th to 16th century atmosphere of the Old Town Market. Even the electric street lights are camouflaged in old-fashioned gas lamp holders.

The authenticity of the restored town was made possible because the Venetian painter Canaletto (mid-18th century) was so taken by the beauty of the square and its surroundings that he left a series of paintings and sketches, filled with exquisite details that guided the feat of reconstruction following World War II. It will be worth your while to visit the National Museum in Warsaw to see the original paintings.

As you look at the square, you may have a feeling of déjà vù, and you will be right. The architecture and layout of the square are quite similar to those visible in most towns of Central and Western Europe, especially Germany. Many of Poland's towns were originally populated by German merchants, artisans and craftsmen, who brought with them the styles, customs, social structures, and city government. Traces of their presence are visible in all Polish towns which date back to the 13th century.

The Jewish migration to Poland's towns and cities followed closely on the heels of the influx of German burghers. Although the Germans were not friendly to the Jews, the language of the Jews, Yiddish, was actually a German dialect with Hebrew and subsequently Polish language additions. Thus the Jews could communicate with the Germans, but had difficulties communicating with the Polish population. (While spoken Yiddish was understandable for a German, written Yiddish was not, because it uses the Hebrew alphabet and is written from right to left.) The difficulty the Jewish people had communicating with the Poles and thus integrating into the Polish culture had far reaching consequences which surfaced time and again throughout the history of Poland.

As a matter of fact, the area around Old Town was at one time inhabited mostly by Jews. If you take a ten-minute stroll from the colorful life-filled Old Town in a western direction you will come face to face with the Ghetto Monument, erected to commemorate the Jewish Uprising of April 1943. The Uprising took place in the ghetto that pre-existed the Nazi occupation of Poland. The Monument marks the place where the Nazis loaded the Jews for transport to death in the ovens of Auschwitz. A stroll in a southerly direction through any one of the store-lined cobbled streets will take you out of Old Town and lead you to the Royal Palace.

The Palace, the square in front of it and the tall monument of King Sigismund III Vasa, which stands close to the center of the square, contain volumes of Poland's history, its glory, its perils, its shame and its heroism.

In mentioning the Royal Palace, and by implication the governance of Poland, it is appropriate to mention that Poland was long the most tolerant kingdom of Europe. Some 75 percent of Europe's Jews chose to live in Poland, where they prospered and developed their culture and learning to the point that Poland's yeshivas (Jewish universities) supplied most of the rabbis for the rest of Europe. The Jews of Poland had their own parliament (the Parliament of the Four Lands) which passed laws, determined the tax rates, etc. Not until the establishment of the State of Israel did the Jews again have their own elected house of representatives.

CHAPTER THREE

Warsaw:
The Story Told by
the Royal Castle

All that remained of the Royal Castle at the end of World War II was a wall, a portion of a tower, and brick outlines of the foundation. Except for a few historians and restoration experts, most of Poland's people were not very interested in rebuilding it. They had good reasons for that feeling, the most important one being that the real Royal Palace is the Wawel in Krakow. That is the palace of Poland's glory, the home of its great royal dynasties, the Piast and the Jagiellonians. Secondly, the Warsavians saw a greater need for investment in much needed housing than in the rebuilding of a palace. The unpopular Communist Regime, however, decided in its everlasting search for legitimacy to rebuild the Royal Castle, hoping to rekindle Polish patriotism with positive effects for the regime. Also, those in power believed that the project would encourage Poles living abroad to contribute to its rebuilding and in that way cooperate for the first time with a regime they genuinely detested. Poles both at home and abroad were social democrats with a sprinkling of capitalists, but they were never communists. Only some minor exceptions, who sought profit from an association with that ideology, aligned themselves with communism. In the case of the castle, however, the Regime was right. The Poles living outside of the country did contribute lavish amounts to the rebuilding of the Royal Castle. Now that it is standing and nearly finished, it has gained acceptance, largely due to the impeccable credentials of Professor Geysztor, custodian of the Castle.

Professor Geysztor is a meticulous historian with a very sharp eye for detail. He and his assistants scoured Poland for proper furnishings, manufactured the correct drapes, used the right paints and gave the interior of the Castle the look it once had, and certainly deserved. Now that the task has been nearly completed—not quite yet to the satisfaction of its custodian—the people have accepted it, even like it and tourists enjoy visiting it. The credit for a job well done is given to the artisans and painters, who frequently worked for very little money, and to the professor. The Regime profited not a wit.

Actually the Regime in its bumbling and authoritarian way has done a lot that would have been praiseworthy had it been done as an expression of the people's will and with good intentions rather than for the perpetuation of the Soviet Communist Regime.

In the consciousness of most Poles, Stalinism and the Russian domination of Poland are synonyms. First Imperial Russia and then Red Russia oppressed Poland and thus Russophobia has become a Polish national disease that even the popular Gorbachev may not be able to cure. The fact that the Russian people suffered as much, if not more than the Poles, has no impact on the attitude toward Russia of an overwhelming number of Poles.

The Royal Palace of Warsaw, from the moment of its construction in the early 17th century to the instant of its destruction in 1944, was never the center of real, effective political power, with the exception of a few brief moments. One of these moments came on the eve of the Second Partition of Poland (1791) among Russia, Prussia and Austria, when Poland's very sophisticated political thought reached its apogee in the promulgation of the Constitution of the Third of May. This constitution combined the best elements to be found in the American Constitution and in the French declaration of The Rights of Man and Citizen. (Incidentally, the debates raging at the Continental Congress in America provoked equally hot debates among the political and intellectual elite of Poland. They learned abut those debates from the French press which circulated among the elite who, like most well-educated Europeans mastered French as their second language.) Yet the Polish Constitution was never implemented. Catherine the Great of Russia, Frederick the Great of Prussia, and the great Maria Theresa of Austria, rightly perceived that the consequences of the Constitution of the Third of May could lead to the re-emergence of a strong Poland and therefore decided to wipe Poland off the map of Europe. For about 150 years there was no Poland, with one short exception during the Napoleonic period when the Emperor created the Duchy of Warsaw, a tiny island of Poland that did not outlast the Emperor.

Prior to the brief moment of constitutional glory which occurred when the Pole Stanislaw August Poniatowski was elected king in 1764, the game concerning the occupant of the Castle was a favorite pre-occupation of Europe's imperial dynasties. The players in the game were the great families of Poland who earned fortunes in bribes by supporting candidates competing for the throne of Poland.

Some of their residences have also been restored and now serve various ministries. You can see them in the vicinity of the Castle. There are fifty-two palaces within the radius of a mile of the palace. Most belonged to the Radziwils, Czartoryskis and Branickis who also owned whole provinces and towns. These palaces, most Baroque in style and very opulent, were destroyed by the Nazis during the Warsaw upris-

ing of 1944. Yet the Communist Regime restored the outside
and housed ministries inside. One of the best examples is the
ornate palace of the Pac family which is now the Ministry of
Health. It is one of those ironies of history that a government
that would have jailed and even executed the legitimate
owners of these palaces rebuilt them to house institutions
which would be much better served by a modern office building. In any event, the fact that they have been restored gives
character to the city and they are definitely tourist attractions.
Sometimes an observant tourist will notice a small plaque
near the foundation of a wall of a restored palace with a name
on it and two dates. The second date will either by 1939 or
1944. These plaques commemorate Polish heroes killed fighting the Germans or executed by them.

The fact that the Polish kings were elected made the Castle
a unique stage for comedies as well as tragedies. The elections
had to be unanimous and a veto of one member of the *szlachta*
would nullify an election or law. This provision was known as
the *liberum veto*. Usually the member of the electorate who
posed the veto did so at the instigation of, and in the interest
of, the magnates, the great families of Poland who as owners
and rulers of entire provinces had an understandably deep
aversion to the emergence of a strong centralized power in
Poland. The *szlachta*, in their service, benefited and could
maintain a life of leisure and indolence. According to the best
estimates dating from the 17th to 18th centuries, about
800,000 Poles were considered to be members of the *szlachta*.
Since there were so many, there was room in that social class
for a significant number of highly educated, dedicated pa-
triots who cared about Poland and its future.

In return for their services, the magnates were richly re-
warded with high court appointments and land grants. The
genuine Polish aristocracy who assisted strong kings in ruling
Poland was an "aristocracy of service." Titles were a reflection
of duties. Thus, for example, the commanding general of an
army was a *hetman* appointed by the king and not some prince
who received the command because he was the son of a
prince. The title *hetman* was not hereditary. For centuries the

szlachta was the pillar of the kingdom's military power and stability.

In the 18th century and even after Poland was partitioned, scions of the great families became what we call in modern parlance "collaborators." Some of their offspring, however, chose different roads and thus saved the honor of some of Poland's most famous names. The partitions impoverished the *szlachta* whose support the princes no longer needed. Many of them left Poland to fight in any army against those who dismembered Poland. They fought as soldiers, as writers, as musicians and poets. They wrote the most outstanding pages of Poland's history. In the span of nearly two centuries the *szlachta* fought on the side of Napoleon on battlefields from Haiti to Moscow. They provoked, participated in and conducted ten rebellions, wars and armed uprisings. On the average, the Poles under *szlachta* leadership fought for freedom once every ten or twenty years. Moreover, the *szlachta* participated in revolutions that took place outside of Poland because its members hoped that a victorious revolution for freedom and democracy in any country would eventually help alleviate the harshness of existence prevailing in Poland.

Most of those rebellions were directed against the foreign powers whose representatives resided in Warsaw's Royal Castle making the rebuilding of the Castle a monument to the determination of the Poles to be independent. In the most recent history of Poland, the greatest clashes between the young activists of Solidarity and the repressive powers of the Communist regime took place in front of the Palace.

CHAPTER FOUR

Warsaw:
The Story Told by
Three
Monuments

If you choose to walk along the left side of the Palace Square
you will be able to see the Vistula River. The Vistula links the
stately old capital of Poland, Krakow, with the more ram-
bunctious new capital of Poland. It completes its flow to the
Baltic Sea at Gdansk, the water exit for Poland's economy, the
proud city which Hitler wanted for his Thousand Year Reich.
Poles in 1939 said "NO," then fought and died for Gdansk,
regained it and made it the heart and symbol of Poland's
struggle to be free. The Solidarity movement was born in the

Lenin Shipyards with the purpose of destroying Leninism in all of its repressive forms.

The Vistula is responsible for the existence of Gdansk. Looking at it from the ramparts of the Palace Square, you will see the narrow parks which frame the river. You will also no doubt observe a few barges passing somnolently, bringing their bulky cargoes to industries along the river. These industries have polluted the river's water with devastating ecological consequences, yet there still are some hardy fishermen, motivated by an irrational hope, who watch their fishing poles for signs that some fish has decided to swim in the Vistula. How different the sight is from the one painted by Canaletto! He saw a river bustling with commercial activity, its waters clear and clean, a Poland that was. Now it is again trying to be.

The Vistula (Wisla, pronounced "Visla") is the aorta through which flows the life blood of Polish history. Like Egypt's Nile, the Vistula is more than a river, it is the "monument" of Poland. It is also the single greatest silent, but inspiring, witness to Poland's proverbial patriotism.

Taking into account only the events that shaped Poland's history in our country, the Vistula has played a decisive role in the fate of Poland. After World War I, when Poland regained the status of an independent nation, the Allies, influenced by a report of Lord Curzon, favored giving vast areas of eastern Poland, inhabited by a majority of Poles, to the Russians. (Incidentally the current eastern borders correspond more or less to the line drawn on the map of Eastern Europe by Curzon.)

The Poles led by Marshal Jozef Pilsudski would not accept the recommendation of the Western Powers and went to war against Bolshevik Russia. The Polish army, and especially the cavalry, made spectacular progress and even occupied Kiev. The Russian counteroffensive proved to be too powerful for the slender Polish army and rolled back the Polish forces to the banks of the Vistula, threatening Warsaw. Despite the pessimism of Allied generals, who observed the war and concluded that Warsaw would fall, Warsaw not only held, but the Polish army was able to go on the counteroffensive and chase the Red armies out of Poland. The events which took place around Warsaw in the summer of 1920 are referred to by Poles as "the Miracle on the Vistula." The Polish counteroffensive succeeded not only in protecting Warsaw, but in forcing the Soviet Union to join a peace conference held in Lithuania's capital, Riga. The peace terms gave Poland most of the provinces in which the majority of the population was Polish.

While only specialists in Polish history know the tortuous negotiations that led to the Riga Treaty, all Poles know about the "Miracle on the Vistula." But Stalin's Russia has a long memory. In August 1944, the magnificently armed and victorious Red Army reached the Eastern banks of the Vistula and were preparing for the final great offensive of World War II. Since there were Polish armed forces fighting alongside the Russians against their common enemy, and since there was a powerful, well organized Polish underground army (known under the cryptonym AK) under the command of the Polish Government in Exile in London, the Home Army chose to undertake the liberation of Warsaw and attacked the elite German SS divisions stationed in Poland's capital. Had they succeeded in liberating Warsaw, the London anti-communist regime would have returned to Poland and Stalin would have never have been able to place his Polish toadies at the head of a liberated Poland.

Look again at the Vistula. Imagine the Polish AK forces controlling a significant part of the river bank and even gaining a foothold on the far bank with Stalin issuing an order that the Red Armies have to cease all offensive operations for the purpose of a regrouping and resupplying their forces. An army a few hundred yards away of the AK watched as the Nazis slowly and methodically butchered the Freedom Fighters and systematically destroyed Warsaw, reducing it into one gray sea of rubble and ruin. The Warsaw uprising lasted from August 1 to October 2, 1944. Some 160,000 civilians were killed and 75 percent of the city completely destroyed. On January 17, 1945, the Red Army liberated Warsaw. For more than five months Stalin watched Warsaw die, because if he had allowed Warsaw to liberate itself, the evil empire would have never come into existence.

There are occasions when platitudes offer valid explana-
tions; "what goes around, comes around." Warsaw 1990 is the
capital of an independent Poland, raising high its traditional
emblem of the eagle with the crown and restoring its right
identity as the Republic of Poland. This too happened on the
banks of the Vistula. Historians of the future may refer to the
events of 1989-90 as the "Second Miracle of the Vistula." In
those two years, people along the Vistula pulled "the rug
from under" the greatest empire of repression and succeeded
in shaking not only one cell of the prison house of nations,
but them all. It was the audacious electrician of Gdansk—Lech
Walesa—guided by the Polish Pope, helped by the intellectuals, and eventually by 80 percent of the Poles, who rang the
bells of liberty and created the symphony of liberty bells
heard all over Eastern and East Central Europe. This time the
symphony will never be silenced.

Look at the river and see and feel, that as strong and steady
as its flow to the sea is, it is but a fit compliment to the spirit of
freedom that fills the very air.

A walk down the broad avenue away from Palace Square is
pleasing to the eye. Shortly you come upon a monument
surrounded by a colorful flower bed in the warmer months.
The man on the top of the monument is Adam Mickiewicz
(1798–1855). Although a Lithuanian by birth, Mickiewicz
(pronounced "Mitzkevitch") was and remains the Poet Laure-
ate of Poland. He was a friend of Pushkin, his counterpart in
Russian literary history, and spent time in a Siberian camp for
his political activities on behalf of a democratic Poland and
Russia. Later he emigrated to Paris, became a professor of
Slavic history and literature at the Sorbonne, and wrote magnificent epic poetry. In 1848, when all of Europe rebelled
against the remnants of absolutism, Mickiewicz feared that
the wave of revolution would engulf Poland and move to
Constantinople (Istanbul) to create a Polish Legion that would
march to help Poland regain freedom. He failed, just as the
Revolutions of 1848 failed, and he died in that distant city. In
the West the Revolutions of 1848 brought about a degree of
liberalization and established the principle of constitutional
monarchy. For a brief moment, even the Poles who rebelled

against Prussia and Austria were on the verge of succeeding in at least the territories occupied by those two powers. The Poles established the Republic of Krakow, but it was an ephemeral structure. Yet 1848 did liberalize the Habsburg Empire (Austria) with the consequence that the Polish land under its domination (mainly Galicia) did benefit and in time became the center of Polish political and cultural life, while serving as a safe haven for Polish and Russian activists escaping the vigilance of the dreaded III Department of the Imperial Russian Secret Police. Anyone captured by its agents was summarily condemned to a long incarceration in the coldest areas of distant Siberia. Among those who found safety in Krakow were Lenin and Stalin. History has its own irony.

Mickiewicz symbolizes the heroic determination of Poland's intelligentsia to protect, enrich, and extend to broader horizons Poland's language and culture. This was not an easy task in an occupied land, especially since the Imperial Russian Government embarked on a policy of Russification of Poland. The stated purpose of that policy was to eliminate the Polish language and stop the evolution of Polish art, music and culture in general. If any Pole wanted to get ahead, he had to learn Russian, graduate from a Russian school, and, if he had serious ambitions, convert to Greek Orthodoxy. In the last decades of the 19th century only a Greek Orthodox could be a good—meaning trustworthy—Russian. Polish schools were closed. Polish newspapers could not be published and the Polish theater ceased to function. The policy failed because of an enormous resistance by the intelligentsia recruited primarily from the ranks of the *szlachta* and supported by the aristocracy and the middle classes. They all wanted to read Mickiewicz and the other great poets. His poetry was patriotic with a strong element of a realistic understanding of Polish history. He was opposed to any repressive regime and especially the Imperial Russian. While summarizing the ethos of Poland, Mickiewicz was and remains the searing flame of the anti-Russian sentiment which persistently surfaces. In 1956, in 1969, and in 1980 the anti-communist, anti-Soviet opposition of Polish intellectuals began under the monument of Mickiewicz. In 1968, a performance of his play "Dziady" (loosely translated as "The Beggars") sparked a demonstration by the audience which escalated quickly into a massive, vociferous opposition to the Polish Communist Government, rightly perceived as a camouflaged extension of Soviet (meaning Russian) domination in Poland.

The Poles succeeded in the defense of their language and culture. The Czechs were less lucky. When their first modern historian Palacky wrote their history, he had to write it in German. The Czech language, surviving among the peasants, was too poor to be used for literary purposes. This, of course, is no longer true, but it proves the point that not even a language can be taken for granted and needs to be protected. In Poland it was, frequently at the risk of imprisonment and exile. For a while, in the mid-19th century, Polish culture really flourished only in emigration—mostly in France—which means Paris. To a lesser degree this is even true today. The cultural affinity of Poland's artists and intellectuals for Paris seems to be a permanent bridge linking the two nations, despite the fact that France had not proved to be a reliable ally of Poland.

A scant few hundred yards from the Monument of Mickiewicz stands the figure of Prince Josef (Joseph) Poniatowski in uniform on horseback. But before you look at it and listen to its story, you may want to cross the street for a little rest. Excellent coffee and pastry can be found in the charming coffee house Telimena, which has been the gathering place of writers and artists for more than a century. Warsaw's coffee houses have many stories to tell, but they can be heard only by those who stay in Poland long enough to learn the language which sounds so harsh to those who do not know it, yet is beautiful, lyrical and very rich. A lot of the most interesting history of modern Poland was born of debates in coffee houses, over a glass of wine and delicious pastry. Coffee houses, with their small marble topped tables and soft chatter of hushed voices are superb places to start a conspiracy, to conclude a somewhat shady deal in order to survive the harsh realities of daily life, to gossip or and to cement a relationship. But, lets get back to monuments.

Prince Jozef Poniatowski (1763–1813) was the commander of the Polish armed forces which fought on the side of Napoleon during a number of crucial battles, the most important ones taking place in the Russian Campaign of 1812. It was Poniatowski's light cavalry that protected the emperor on his flight from Russia and it was Poniatowski's soldiers who perished with their commander at the battle of Lipsk, in which the anti-Napoleonic alliance defeated the emperor and eventually forced his resignation.

The monument to Poniatowski symbolizes Poland's love affair with Napoleon—this son of the French Revolution, this conqueror of Europe, was perceived to be the eventual liberator of Poland. The hope was not without reason because Napoleon had decisively defeated Austria, Prussia and Russia, the three powers who had engineered the partitions of Poland and occupied the land.

From the very beginnings of Napoleon's career, Polish legionnaires fought on his side. They were recruited from among the Poles who escaped their occupied homeland and were augmented by large numbers of *szlachta* and peasants. They fought under the command of General Dambrowski in every major battle waged by Napoleon, especially when his armies were in dangerous positions. One of the most famous exploits of the Polish cavalry was to charge through the Somosierra Pass, which blocked Napoleon's march to Madrid. There was no Polish Lord Tennyson to immortalize this famous and equally foolhardy charge of the light brigade, but there should have been. The prize for all of the human sacrifice was a promise to liberate Poland.

In fact, Napoleon did create the Duchy of Warsaw in 1807, which included Krakow. He imposed a constitution and the Napoleonic Code of Laws, which to this date is the basis of Polish jurisprudence (also in Louisiana). The duchy survived until 1815, when Napoleon suffered his ultimate defeat at Waterloo and was exiled to St. Helena. The duchy, with some territorial adjustments (notably the transfer of Krakow back to the Austrians), survived as the Congress Kingdom ruled by Czar Alexander I, who crowned himself king of Poland. The effective rule was passed on to Crown Prince Constantin, brother of the czar. The Congress Kingdom (It got this name because it was created by the Congress of Vienna which redrew the map of Europe in order to undo the political confusion created by Napoleon.) lasted until 1830. The Poles had a substantial degree of autonomy including a small armed force. In November 1830, the Poles rebelled against the Russian rule, were defeated and for all practical purposes, from 1830 until the Soviet Revolution of 1917, Russia's Polish provinces were referred to as the "Lands along the Vistula." The object of Alexander's successors was to change their part of Poland into a subservient and culturally integrated part of the Russian empire. The current Russophobia of the Poles has deep roots.

To this day the Polish national anthem, formerly a marching song of Napoleon's Polish legions, is the only national anthem that glorifies Napoleon in its lyrics. "Bonaparte showed us how we have to win," it says. The Bonaparte who callously used the Poles to further his imperial designs is still perceived by many Poles as a daring and successful architect of modern European history. The loyalty of Poniatowski, who refused to betray his commander-in-chief after even his closest friends and family left and his fortunes dimmed, is typical of the outstanding concept of honor cherished by the *szlachta*. The reckless cavalry charge of Somosierra is embedded in the ethos of the country as a symbol of courage. It is difficult to hear the voices of moderation in a country whose history has been written by poets and political dreamers.

The three monuments will always be cherished by Poles, but now they have acquired a different aura. They are no longer revered as symbols of Poland's resistance to communism, but now offer a rallying point for nationalism, with all of its dreams, bigotry, and cultural chauvinism. The transition from a Soviet-type economy to a "free market economy" is not easy, but the healthy Polish nationalism is fostering a sense of civil responsibility for the well being of the country as a whole, which demands social justice, and whose tenor is most akin to the ethos represented by the three monuments.

CHAPTER FIVE

Warsaw: The Story Told by the Church of the Holy Cross and Chopin's Heart

If you had the good fortune to have a window seat on the plane that brought you to Warsaw, you would have noticed the great number of church steeples. The predominance of churches is a distinguishing feature of Poland's cities and country villages. Poland has three symbols: the eagle, the crown and the cross. The eagle seems to be the bird of preference in most European countries. The crown, although present in other national symbols, has a special meaning for Poles; it belongs to the Virgin Mary, Queen of Poland. She was elevated to this status in 1717, the year of the famous defense of Czestochowa by a handful of Poles against the Swedes, who occupied nearly all of Poland. The Polish forces defended the Monastery of Czestochowa and every day paraded the ikon of the Virgin Mary and prayed for help. The Poles succeeded and the Swedish army soon thereafter had to evacuate all of their forces from Poland. The grateful Piarist fashioned a golden crown and placed it on the head of the Virgin Mary, who from that time on is referred to as the Queen of Poland.

Poland's first national anthem "Mother of God, by God Blessed Maria" was sung by Polish knights fighting the Tutons in the 14th century. During the recent (1980-1989) struggles for freedom and relief from communism, the hymn acquired a special meaning. It became a protest song of Solidarity and the unofficial national anthem. The Virgin Mary and the cross are never far from the center of Poland's culture and history. Though this fact does not mean that the Poles are especially religious, it does mean that they are devoted to symbols which have acquired a special meaning through history. The composer of the "Mother of God" hymn is unknown.

Nearly all the churches in Warsaw are baroque in style. What is most striking about them and visible in the majority of the Catholic churches in Poland is that the Virgin Mary occupies the commanding position behind the altar. Christ is usually relegated to a position to the right of His Mother as you face the altar. The close identification of about 95 percent of the Polish people with the Virgin Mary is understandable considering the centuries of suffering of the people. The Virgin Mary is both the Mother Dolorosa (the Suffering Mother) and the One who is full of grace and love and can intercede with the Son to help His people, to make life more bearable, and more secure. The Virgin Mary is Poland's symbol of eternal hope.

The Church of the Holy Cross is just a few minutes walk

down the street from the Poniatowski monument. On the way to the church you will pass the University of Warsaw which has a fascinating history. The University evolved gradually. At the very back of the campus is an elegant small palace which served as a school for military cadets. Its most famous alumnus was Kosciuszko. If you go to the English Department at the university, you can certainly find a student who would gladly give you a guided tour. Inquire at the office marked "Secretariat." Young Poles are eager to practice their English.

To get to the church, you have to cross the street known today as Nowy Swiat (New World). In front of the church is a figure of Christ bent under the weight of the cross He must bear. Inside the church, in a special ornate urn, is the heart of Frederick Chopin, who requested that his heart be buried in the land to which most of his music was dedicated.

Chopin put into music the beauty and joy, the soft melancholy of the Polish countryside, its people, its history. To this day his mazurkas, polonaises and sonatas stir the patriotic feelings of many Poles. Three notes of his polonaise are particularly famous; they were used by Radio Warsaw as its musical signature. In 1939, when the German army besieged Warsaw, Poles knew that as long as they heard those three notes, Warsaw had not yet fallen. After seventeen days of heroic fighting the notes went off the air. In 1942, when the entire European continent was occupied by the Nazis, the British Broadcasting Company used the first cord of Beethoven's Fifth Symphony to alert all resistance movements that the news program was about to begin. The BBC was the only daily contact the forces fighting against Hitler had. If Hitler's henchmen caught anyone listening to it, he was incarcerated, and likely as not, ended in a concentration camp.

Chopin's music echoed the hope of Poles in Paris awaiting the day they could return home. Like Mickiewicz's poetry, Chopin's music served as the constant reminder that Poland was alive, that it existed and that it would be free. While Chopin could not return to Poland, his polonaise and mazurkas were the favorite dance music at all the courts of Europe, including the courts of Vienna, Berlin and St. Petersburg—the courts of those who really wanted to permanently erase all vestiges of the Polish nation. Conquerors never learn that as long as a nation's art remains alive, the nation remains alive.

Yet, in Poland, the Vatican Church, always so quick to proclaim Poland "the shield of Christendom," was silent when Poland was being oppressed and hundreds of priests perished. The popes counseled obedience to the crowns, obedience to the laws of the occupiers, and did nothing to help the Polish people. They gave their faith to the Virgin Mary Queen of Poland.

It's time for a lunch break. After that we will go to Wilanow, the park and Royal Palace built by Jan Sobieski for his beloved Marysia (little Mary). Sobieski was the Polish king who in 1863 defeated the mightiest army of the Ottoman (Turkish) Empire when it was about to conquer Vienna and disrupt to the heart of Europe.

To have a good lunch before your visit to Wilanow, go to the Victoria Intercontinental. Rich or poor, the Poles like to eat well and a lot. They eat their lunches late, usually between 2 and 4 PM. For many, lunch is the main meal of the day. Most will eat at their work places, which maintain dining facilities. Some, who work for American or Western companies and thus are very well paid, will eat in restaurants like the one in the Victoria. In short, lunch is a production. The menu at the Victoria consists of appetizers washed down with vodka, a main course of meat, mountains of potatoes, salads, and a dessert and an expresso to finish. While the dining room is very comfortable, and the table settings appealing, the service is competent, but slow. A lunch may take about two hours.

The way around this is to have lunch in the breakfast room. The menu may be more restricted, but the service is faster. You can order tasty chicken and tuna salads, or the Polish version of the hamburger which is a *sznycel* (shnitzel) of either chopped veal or beef served with french fried potatoes. A specialty of Poland is a Steak Tartar, as described earlier. It is delicious, but should only be eaten in first class restaurants. A shot of vodka is a wonderful accompaniment along with the crusty black bread. You can also have a sandwich, which in Poland is called "a toast." In the fish category, we highly recommend trout, salmon (smoked) or carp in jelly and herring. Frequently Beluga caviar is also on the menu. Our suggestion is that you eat the light lunch and reserve your feasting for the evening meal. There is no night life to speak of, so an evening feast is the best substitute. The evening menu will be richer and take longer to consume.

After you have had your light meal, get a taxi and go to Wilanow (Vilanov). The palace built by Sobieski is a miniature Versailles, set in the middle of a charming formal garden. It has been restored and the garden is kept in excellent shape. The area where the king kept his retinue has been utilized to house two superb restaurants, one maintained by Orbis, the second, smaller one is more intimate and privately owned. Either has very good food. The service is better in the private restaurant, yet the selections are better in the Orbis restaurant. Within the park, you will also find Europe's only museum of posters, which is worth a special return trip to Wilanow. The museum contains a fabulous collection of the best works of Europe's outstanding graphic artists, among whom the Poles excel. There are some prints for sale, though originals are unavailable.

Jan (John) the III Sobieski (1624–1696) was elected king of Poland in 1674. He was a patron of the arts, encouraged education, and above all, was a military genius and astute diplomat. He fought a series of successful battles with the Turks forever threatening Poland's southeastern provinces, made peace with the Russians and was generally a Francophile, at a time when the Austrian Habsburgs were attempting to gain influence in Sobieski's court. Despite the fact that Sobieski's beloved wife was a descendant of French royalty, Sobieski allied himself with the Austrian Emperor Leopold I to fight the Turks, at that time termed the Infidels. He was assisted in making this decision by Pope Innocent XI, who actually promoted the idea of a crusade against the Ottoman Empire. The Infidels, however, had a powerful army led by their most experienced vizier, General Kara Mustafa. His forces besieged Vienna and the emperor asked Sobieski for help. On the 12th of September, 1683, the battle to save Vienna began. The Turks had an army of 125,000, the combined Austrian-Polish forces numbered 76,000. The Polish contingent consisted of 25,000, mostly cavalry. Among them were the heavily armed Winged Hussars. They were so named because on the back of their armor they had two rows of eagles' feathers. They were an awesome and fear-inspiring sight. It was the charge of these hussars that finally broke through the ranks of the elite Turkish troops and captured the tent of Kara Mustafa, who fled the battlefield. Vienna was saved and the Ottoman Empire never again threatened the safety of all Europe. Sobieski, upon entering Vienna, paraphrased Caesar saying, *Veni Vidi Deus Vicit* (I came, I saw, God won). Sobieski was a devout Catholic. He remained the pope's strongest ally. The armor of the hussars, and the grand vizier's tent are on display at the Museum of the Armed Forces located at the center of Warsaw. It is an interesting place to visit and to get a real sense of Poland's glory.

Sobieski was a very tolerant king and a great protector of the Jewish population, which made him an exception among the rulers of Europe. Yet the most touching aspect of his personality was his love for his wife Marysienka, a love which she reciprocated. Their devotion to each other has been eternalized by their common grave which stands in the Wilanow park. It is a very imposing monument with the sculpture of the pair lying under an ornate canopy.

Sobieski did not rule from the Royal Palace, and when he mobilized his army to march to the rescue of Vienna, he issued the call from Krakow, the old capital. This king truly belongs to the great tradition of Poland, and his death is the epilogue to Poland's place as one of Europe's great powers.

CHAPTER SIX

Warsaw: The City and How to Enjoy All It Has to Offer

We are firm believers that the best way to see a city is to walk through those areas that provide the greatest aesthetic pleasures, as well as a few that are of particular significance to the permanent residents. We suggest that you take a taxi to the area you want to see and then walk around.

If you stay in either Warsaw's Holiday Inn or the Novotel, take a taxi to the Place of Three Crosses, so named because there is a church and two crosses on the square. From there enter the Aleje Ujazdowskie (pronounced "Ooyazdovske").

Pass by a few of the magnificent pre-war apartment buildings, spared destruction during the Home Army (AK) uprising because the entire area was occupied by high German officials and the Nazis had no desire to destroy their own homes and offices. The Home Army, on the other hand, could not spare the forces to break through the iron ring of the German defenses. The Aleje was not a primary objective for the Freedom Fighters.

This broad avenue is Warsaw's showcase of elegance. The single glaring exception to it is the American Embassy, which the wits of Warsaw, have dubbed "the refrigerator lying on its side." The description fits. The embassy is a rectangular, modernistic box of small windows and blue siding. It is absolutely devoid of grace, as are the buildings that house the personnel.

All the buildings along the Aleje Ujazdowskie are on the right hand side. Most of the buildings are former palaces converted either into embassies or into housing for the most important institutions of the Polish Government. The left side of the Aleje marks the boundary of Warsaw's most beautiful park, the Lazienkowski Garden, named after the architectually most beautiful palace of Warsaw, which stands in the middle of the garden on the banks of an artificial lake. The Lazienkowski Palace is a small jewel. The park is well laid out, beautifully maintained and its cleanliness, like the cleanliness of most of Warsaw's main streets, provokes a feeling of envy, especially among tourists from large American cities. The park is sufficiently wide to dampen the noises of the city and provides a cool area for talk, contemplation, reading or simply relaxing. There is a cafe in the park and the Polish ice cream served there is delicious and fresh. The wooden benches are well maintained and the people whom you will encounter are polite and friendly.

The greatest fun for us was to watch the well-nourished, happy kids doing their kid stuff. As you reach the end of the park you come upon the Polish White House, the residence of Poland's president, known as the Belweder. This palace is surrounded by the usual security walls and security personnel, and frankly, it rivals the U.S. Embassy in its beauty, despite its non-descript mixture of classical and baroque style. A short distance from the Belweder is the massively imposing Soviet Embassy, squatting in its neo-classical splendor on a low hill. It can not be seen well from the street because the entire space is surrounded by a huge wall.

There are no shops on the Aleje Ujazdowskie, yet when seen in its imposing perspective, it justifies a visit.

Across the street, a little bit to the left of the American Embassy, is the restaurant aptly named The Ambassador. It also has a separate coffee house. The restaurant offers good food of average quality—mostly traditional Polish dishes. If you are in luck they may serve a tasty pork cutlet. The coffee house has very good pastry, good coffee and snacks. It's a good place to rest after a long walk. A little bit down the street in the direction of the Place of Three Crosses and across the street from the Ambassador is one of Warsaw's rowdiest and most famous institutions, the SPATIF. The name is an acronym for the club of Polish actors, writers, and assorted literati. Technically you can not walk in if you are not a member of one of those professions, but if you do, no one will ask any questions. The club has excellent food and all sorts of drinks which are consumed in imposing quantities. What makes the club interesting is that you do meet Poland's outstanding actors, producers, and screen writers, most of whom speak English. In the ambiance of the club, when you are fortified by a good scotch, the conversation flows freely and could give you an insight, an understanding, of the mind set, aspirations and hopes of Poland's creative people, free for the first time in half a century to articulate their imagination. Don't be bashful about buying people drinks and accepting their invitations to visit them. They embroider their stories, but after all. . . .

One morning you must walk down Warsaw's main drag—the Marshal's Avenue—Ulica Marszalkowska. It was completely rebuilt from the ground up after World War II. The buildings trace in their style Poland's escape from Stalinist domination. At the mid-point of the avenue stands the Palace of Culture, Stalin's gift to the Polish people, a building so ponderously ugly that it deserves to bear his name—it still does, in fake gold, barely visible over the massive doors. At

one time, it was the tallest building in Warsaw, clearly visible
from all districts of the city. The central tower is connected to
four appendages, a theater, a movie house, an assembly hall,
and to one of the lowest, malodorous night clubs to be found
anywhere in Europe. The interior of the building is marble,
crystal, and bronze, designed to convey the feeling of perma-
nence. The exterior has porticos and friezes supported by
imitation Grecian columns. Atop the appendages, the roofs
are garlanded by concrete vines and other creeping vegetation. This Palace of Culture stands in the middle of a stone
desert for which the Warsaw city fathers have never been able
to find a use.

The building is the home of the Polish Academy of Science,
which now has gained the luster such an institution deserves.
On the ground floor is an excellent bookstore worth browsing
through.

In the fall the "stone desert" blooms when peasants exhibit
their colorful folk art and booksellers hold an outdoor exhibit.

For forty years Warsaw's inventive and creative architects
have been trying to hide the palace by surrounding it with
taller buildings, huge department stores, restaurants and
cinemas. With the completion of the new Warsaw Marriott, it
seems they have finally succeeded.

Fascinating for tourists interested in shopping is a series of
small shops within a five-minute walk from the palace. Everything from furs to designer dresses and silk ties can be purchased from courteous vendors. And to prove that Warsaw
did join the high-tech age, there is a store with every imagin-
able gadget that can be found on 42nd Street in New York
City.

The avenue is very broad and used by all means of transportation: trolleys, buses, taxis, and unending streams of
rushing people. The big stores offer nothing that could interest Americans, and if you do wish to go inside, there is a long
line of customers waiting their turn to be allowed in. You
would do better to continue walking until you come to Constitution Place, one of the best examples of Stalinist architecture to be found anywhere in Eastern Europe. There is no
sense describing it; you have to inhale its atmosphere, imag-

ine the self importance of the Stalinist thugs who lived in the nearby apartments, and the fear inspired by the offices surrounding the square. The square was to be the vision of the ultimate classless society. Actually it is a poor imitation of a cheap Hollywood set, supposedly replicating the grandeur of the Roman Empire, with Napoleon thrown in for good measure.

Our suggestion is that you see the rest of Warsaw by driving around for one day. Use the driver as your guide, or take one of the many brochures available at your hotel and make your own choices. There are only two recommendations we will make. You should see the Jewish Cemetery because many of the names on the grave stones will sound familiar and give you an inkling of the Jewish contribution to culture and commerce. And at that cemetery you will understand what Poland as a country, a culture, and a people lost in the Holocaust. The second cemetery you should visit is Powazki, the Polish equivalent of Arlington Cemetery. You will see two rows of huge rough-hewn wooden crosses commemorating the fighters who died in the Warsaw Uprising. You will be touched and you will experience heroism.

On the lighter side, you should convince your driver to take you across to the Eastern bank of the Vistula. Ask him to show you the villas, the Washington Circle, and then take you to the section known as Praga. This area survived the war relatively undamanged because the Red Army occupied it before the the Nazis had the chance to destroy it.

Praga was always a workers' district. The buildings date from the end of the 19th century and are similar in style and smell to the Lower East Side tenements prior to gentrification. The restaurants, the bars, the gathering places, the dress and the faces of the inhabitants are living daguerreotypes of yellowing photographs you might find rummaging through your grandparents' attic. When you think about roots, you will remember this place.

At the heart of the district is the best example of 19th century liberal capitalism, a free market. You can find everything that you can not find in the rest of Poland, except at other open air markets of which there are hundreds throughout the country. There is Russian caviar supplied by Soviet train personnel on their stopover in Warsaw. There is gold, there are emerald dealers, there are real and phony designer clothes, there is meat and there are sausages in abundance. There are furs, and there are sections that would do credit to K-Mart. The prices are subject to negotiations, and you will lose no matter how cheaply the merchandise is sold. Most of it was never bought to begin with. The police know it, but this open market, like the others, is a safety valve for a population starved for consumer goods. Be sure your driver goes with you. Chances are he will know which stands are worth going to and he will protect you from the army of pickpockets and inebriated merchants who have already made their profit for the day and are celebrating. The market is on a field which seems to be muddy all the time. Dress accordingly. Have fun and buy something: a fur cap for the equivalent of five dollars, 500 grams of caviar for $25, or a real $20 gold piece for $18. That is one of the many mysteries of the Polish economy: gold selling below the world market price.

The open markets are always crowded, all over Poland. You can ask the legitimate question: How can a country as poor as Poland is alleged to be, have people who can afford to buy so much? The answer is astounding. There is somewhere between $3 billion and $5 billion held privately by Poles (mostly by peasants and entrepreneurs). Now go back to your capitalist hotel, contemplate your loot and rest.

Like all great capitals of Europe, Warsaw has its museums. For us, however all of Warsaw is one vast museum, a real phoenix risen from the ashes. Considering that Poland has been free for only two decades in this century and is now entering on the third, it is remarkable that the people have retained a vitality and a pulsating imagination visible in all the creative arts.

Everyone is aware of the horrors of the Nazi occupation. The Holocaust can never be forgotten and never will be. But few people think of a cultural holocaust, a deliberate policy to destroy all vestiges of Polish poetry, music, architecture and above all history. In the Nazi schema, the Slavs were to be the slaves of the Thousand Year Reich. The Nazis plundered all that was valuable and burned all that was significant. And when they were defeated, the Red Czar—Stalin—was forcing Poland's culture into the sausage-like casing of Leninism-Stalinism. Only those expressions of creativity that fit the ideological parameters of socialist realism and dialectical materialism received official support and funding.

Yes, it is true that Stalin's toadies who ruled Poland allowed the reconstruction of palaces, buildings of significance and even monuments, but these were facades behind which the Red elite was systematically falsifying Poland's history and Poland's contributions to European culture. The sole protector of Poland's culture was the Roman Catholic Church and especially one man, the Prymas of Poland, Stefan Cardinal Wyszynski. His biography is a "must" reading for those who really want to understand the source of survival of culture in Poland. When we go to Poland—to a different region each time—we are constantly reminded that without the steadfast policy of Cardinal Wyszynski much of what we admire now would not have survived in its purity. And without the miracle of a Polish Pope, the Polish people would not have regained freedom in the last decade of this millennium. The Church did not have the monopoly of courage and patriotism, but without the Church the crown would have not been replaced on the white eagle of Poland's real independence. The one proud element of that has gone up in flames and is lost forever is the culture of the Jews. Nowhere is this more evident than in Warsaw.

The usual masterpieces that are found in the great museums and palaces of Europe were looted by the Germans and the Russians. Some of these treasures were returned by the Germans and a few have trickled back from the Soviets. There is hope now that more will be returned by them, because there seems to be a different wind blowing from the east.

With this in mind we do recommend that you visit the National Museum and the Museum of the Polish Army. Both are located on the Aleje Jerozolimskie (pronounced "Aleye

Yerozolimske") in the center of Warsaw. Hopefully the current regime will have the money to uncreate and display the art that was not approved by the previous government. In your hotel you will find English language brochures which provide the details.

CHAPTER SEVEN

A Respite from the 20th Century

Warsaw is emotionally and physically draining. The night before you leave you have to decide how you want to escape the entire 20th century, not only the Polish version, but all of it. You have the unique opportunity to return to pre-industrial revolution Europe filled with the sights and sounds and smells your grandparents may remember from their childhoods. The escape routes are open in all directions of the compass. The choice you have to make is if you prefer the mountains, the seashore, the lakes, or the bucolic country of wheat and corn and lazy rivers.

Whatever you decide, you will always have the option of jumping into 20th century comfort—well-cooked food, clean lodgings, and kind people willing to help you enjoy your stay.

It is hard to believe but thirty miles outside the city limits of any Polish city you will find the 19th century, its slow pace, its respect for nature's timetable to dictate what work needs to be done and when. The typical American twenty-four-hour economy does not even exist as a concept and the rhythm of life is adjusted to the demands of nature and not profit making. Your life will really "dance to a different tune." It took us awhile to become used to the stillness of the night, broken only occasionally by the barking of a dog. It was really too quiet to fall asleep.

Our suggestion is that you start exploration of Poland by taking day trips and return to your Warsaw hotel for the night. The hotel will provide you with a delicious picnic lunch and you can get a mini-bus to your destination. Of course, it's better if you have your own driver, who will stop when you find a picturesque place for a quiet, cool rest. The use of day trips gives you the chance to "test the waters" and see how you like the pace of an earlier time.

We have a preference for the southern and southeastern regions of Poland. The mountains, pine forests and rapidly cascading rivers are magnificent. Then there is the ever changing beauty of the sea and the romantic calm of weeping willows lazily brushing the shores of placid lakes. Both are the real treasures of Poland, but during a two-week trip it is impossible to truly enjoy both. You can see all if you are the tourist version of a jogger and count your accomplishments by miles covered per day. But that is not the reason for a vacation anywhere, and certainly not in Poland. No one drinks a heady vintage wine at a gulp. If you could extend your vacation for one more week, then you could have the best of all possible worlds.

As your first day trip, we highly recommend the Kampinos Forest, which the Poles named the Kampinos Jungle. It offers picturesque walks between marshes, dunes and dense forests. It was once dominated by wild boars, and there still are some, but you would not encounter them. Elk and roe deer you are certain to see. The park is well worth a two-hour walk. Be sure to wear high top sneakers or boots, carry a light jacket and take an insect repellent with you. Mosquitoes, like Gypsies, recognize no frontiers.

The Kampinos Jungle served as a hiding place for Polish

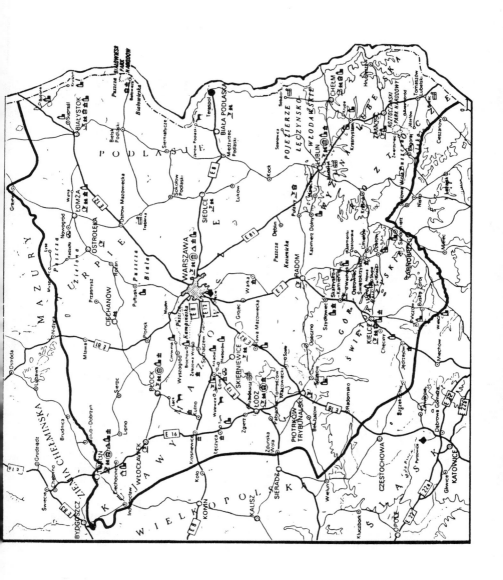

63

partisans in their continuous struggle against the Nazis. The partisans were the Polish version of Robin Hood and his Saxon bands. Only the identity of the evil Sheriff of Nottingham changed.

From Campinos, which is just at the outskirts of Warsaw, you should draw a semi-circle of fifty miles covering the eastern, southern, and perhaps part of the western region around the city. In this way you will have the chance to see the magnificent palace of the Raziwils in Nieborow. The palace is now an extension of the National Museum and some of its rooms are reserved for use by writers and artists who need a quiet place to think, reflect or simply rest. The public rooms are filled with art works: paintings, sculptures and outstanding examples of folk art. The palace, built in the Baroque style, features a staircase of such grandeur and sheer elegance that you will wish you could walk down it in sumptuous evening attire and glittering jewelry. The unusual site is the magnificent library filled with exquisitely bound books; it does justice to a library of an exclusive liberal arts college. The Radziwils have an astounding history of which this palace is but one piece.

On your "must see" list you have to include a visit to Zelazowa Wola, the birthplace of Frederick Chopin. The house in which he was born is modest, small, and very, very attractive. Part of the reason for this is the wonderful gardens that surround it. Some of them are formal, evidently designed by a professional gardener; others are wild, designed by nature. The Chopin residence is superbly maintained and features a salon which contains a Steinway grand piano. From June until September, every Sunday a piano virtuoso plays Chopin's compositions. The music flows out through the large windows and glass doors to the audience sitting in the park. Listening to Chopin's romantic and nostalgic music in this setting adds an extra dimension. In a really mysterious way the setting explains the emotions the music contains.

A twenty-minute drive takes you from Zelazowa Wola to the little town of Lowicz where you can become acquainted with the other spectrum of Poland's culture, that of the peasants. Lowicz has a museum of peasant costumes and folk art of outstanding beauty created by the masterful blending of colors and styles. And that really is enough for a day in another century.

After this one day trip you have an inkling of what you can do and enjoy during a trip to Poland. You obviously have choices. In this book we will tell you in some detail what we think you ought to see and do, but you must decide what it is that your real preferences are. Tourists usually go to Poland for two or three weeks and we want to help you make the most of your stay. Your options are to see the fascinating towns of Poland.

The most important one is Krakow, the city so famous that it is classified by UNESCO (The United Nations institution) as a cultural treasure of Europe. Even the Nazis in retreating from Krakow and the Red Armies on their last great offensive agreed to declare Krakow an open city and not bomb it. Only Rome and Paris have been granted the same status. The other city is Gdansk, Poland's famous port on the Baltic estuary of the Vistula.

World War II began because Poland refused to surrender Gdansk to Nazi domination in 1939. The city was destroyed and lovingly reconstructed. In most recent times it was the dock workers of Gdansk who created the Solidarity movement that began the task of democratizing East-Central Europe. If you have only two weeks, a tour of Warsaw, Krakow, and Gdansk with their environs is a fascinating vacation. But not everyone is a city buff, and some of you actually would prefer the 19th century aspects of rural life in Poland which includes the chance to engage in a variety of sports like mountain climbing, fishing, hunting, kayaking, and horseback riding. (The latter offers riding trails lasting a few days.) If you happen to go to Poland during the winter months, and especially in the period from mid-February to the end of March, you can enjoy all of the winter sports, from skiing to iceboat racing.

We will describe most of these options, but our experience is that you can not squeeze in all of them during just one visit. It becomes too exhaustive and nerve wracking. We believe that one of the charms of vacationing is to be able to follow

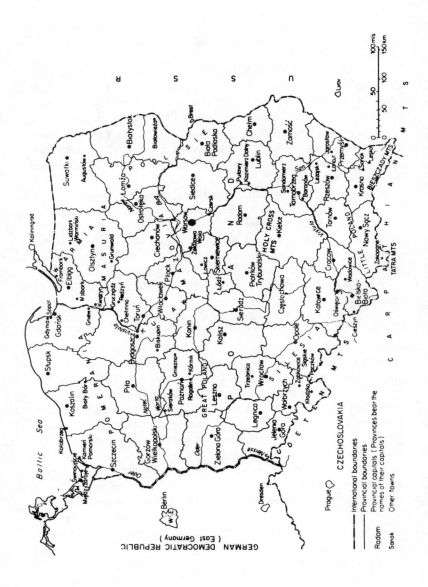

GERMAN DEMOCRATIC REPUBLIC
(East Germany)

CZECHOSLOVAKIA

Prague

International boundaries
Provincial boundaries
Provincial capitals (Provinces bear the
names of their capitals)
Other towns

Radom

Sanok

0   50   100   150 km
0   50   100 mls

Baltic Sea

P O M E R A N I A

M A S U R I A

M A Z O V I A

G R E A T   P O L A N D

S I L E S I A

LITTLE POLAND

HOLY CROSS MTS

SUDETEN MTS

CARPATHIAN MTS

BIESZCZADY MTS

TATRA MTS

HIGH BESKID

U   S   S   R

Kaliningrad
Gdańsk
Gdynia
Sopot
Słupsk
Koszalin
Kołobrzeg
Kamień Pomorski
Szczecin
Świnoujście
Międzyzdroje
Białogard
Piła
Gorzów Wielkopolski
Zielona Góra
Jelenia Góra
Legnica
Wałbrzych
Kłodzko
Ząbkowice Śląskie
Paczków
Zgorzelec
Wrocław
Trzebnica
Leszno
Poznań
Rogalin
Kórnik
Gniezno
Sieraków
Bydgoszcz
Biskupin
Konin
Kalisz
Sieradz
Częstochowa
Opole
Oświęcim
Cieszyn
Bielsko-Biała
Katowice
Kraków
Wadowice
Nowy Sącz
Zakopane
Tarnów
Kielce
Radom
Łódź
Skierniewice
Łowicz
Płock
Włocławek
Wocławek
Toruń
Chełmno
Grudziądz
Kwidzyn
Gniew
Wąbrzeźno
Grunwald
Iława
Malbork
Elbląg
Frombork
Wilbork
Olsztyn
Lidzbark Warmiński
Ciechanów
Ostrołęka
Łomża
Suwałki
Augustów
Białystok
Białowieża
Brześć
Biała Podlaska
Siedlce
Warsaw
Żelazowa Wola
Piotrków Trybunalski
Pułtusk
Chełm
Zamość
Lublin
Kazimierz Dolny
Puławy
Sandomierz
Tarnobrzeg
Baranów
Łańcut
Łańcut
Rzeszów
Leżajsk
Krosno
Jasło
Przemyśl
Sanok
Lvov
San
Wisła
Odra
Warta
Noteć
Bóbr
Nysa

Berlin
Dresden

Baltic Sea

your own schedule. If you do find an enchanting spot, you can stay there a day longer and not worry about having to rush to the next place. If you choose the city tour, you still will see a lot of the countryside and get a fairly comprehensive picture of Poland. But you will not be able to really enjoy and benefit from the tranquillity of the countryside or engage in the sports.

Either choice is good. Either choice is fun. In the pages that follow we will tell you what you can expect. We made one assumption and that is that you will hire a car and a driver for your sojourn in Poland. Relying on public transport is a nightmare. This luxury will cost you $120 to $150 per day. If you speak Polish, you can rent a car for as low as $110 per week. The reason we recommend car rentals only for those who know the language is based on the fact that when something goes wrong with the car, if you do not know the language, you may find it difficult to find a service station and explain what is wrong, and you will not know how to ask for directions or find the right place to stay unless you speak Polish.

Perhaps just one excursion to the environs of Warsaw was not enough to help you decide what you want to see. We did not know either so we decided to go northeast to the town of Bialystok. It took us a little more than two hours to get there.

Bialystok is well known, not only because it produced the best leather manufactured in Poland, but also because so many Jewish families migrated from there to the United States. The famous bialy with cream cheese originated in Bialystok. The city also has examples of magnificent architecture, a legacy of the Branicki magnates who really owned that part of Poland. Close to Bialystok is the Bialowieza National Park, designated by UNESCO as part of network of biosphere reserves. It is truly magnificent, the home of the famous bisons, cousins of the American buffalo, and also the area where an especially flavorful buffalo grass grows. One helm of that flavorful grass placed in a bottle of alcohol creates Poland's truly best drink, the Zobrowka. It is in such great demand that it is difficult to find even in stores which cater only to tourists who can pay in hard, meaning convertible, currency. These stores are known under the acronym Pewex.

While you are driving to whatever destination you chose, stop and look at the still prevailing wooden houses, barns, and occasional churches. Notice that frequently at road crossings you will see small chapels, altars to the Virgin Mary, and a straw-roofed tiny lean-to in which you will find the figure of a very tired, sad, resting Christ.

Notice the peasant women working in the fields, harvesting vegetables, potatoes, and frequently gathering hay and placing it in stacks. Each village or region has a very specific style of a haystack. The women, when they pass a crossroad, will make the sign of the cross to affirm their faith. Your driver, proud of his car, will often grumble at the heavily laden horse-drawn wagons with rubber tires ambling down arterial highways. They are determined to outlast even the Mercedes.

The women, dressed in long black skirts and work-a-day blouses, are in fact the force and the stability of the small family farms which criss-cross the Polish countryside. The men do the heavy work of plowing, fertilizing the land, and transporting the goods to the market. It is the women who do the selling, who hold the purse strings and keep the family intact. They love their men and they give them the outward signs of respect due them in a basically "macho" society. But the women are the strength of Poland's private sector agricultural economy which, in practical terms, means 80 percent of all that Poland produces. The food shortages are due to the lack of adequate transportation from the farm to the market, the catastrophical shortage of refrigerated warehousing, and a totally untenable pricing system.

The crippling shortages, mismanagement and artificial price supports are currently being dismantled by Poland's non-communist government. This is a complex and monumental task which in the beginning will cause confusion and perhaps even greater imbalances in the agrarian sector. In time, however, the reforms and changes will return Poland to the ranks of food exporting countries, a position Poland traditionally enjoyed.

You should make an attempt to spend a Sunday morning in

one of these peasant hamlets and watch the families go to Mass. If you are lucky, the Sunday may fall on a holiday or a special saint's day and you will see the women and their children dressed in their finery. Colorful hand-embroidered costumes will dazzle you and the twenty dollar gold pieces worn as necklaces will amaze you. The children will also wear clean, expensive clothing. The men, on the other hand, will look awkward in their ill-fitting store-bought suits and pointed shoes. If a man sports a colorful sweater, it means one of two things: He either had the chance to work in America or Western Europe or had some relative from the U.S. send a package. On rare occasions men will also dress up in their folkloric costumes and then they too are resplendent.

But what you will enjoy most is taking your picnic basket out into the fields. Find a haystack or a shady tree and drink in the quiet and the peace. Let your imagination carry you wherever it wants. You might even find yourself feeling that you don't have a care in the world.

Two or three daytrips from Warsaw will give you the flavor of the countryside and its unusual architecture of thatched roof wooden houses, artistically adorned barn doors, and the well sculptured woodwork.

A word of caution is called for. Peasant children drink milk as it comes from the cow; they seem immune to the natural bacteria it contains. Americans are used to pasteurized milk and have no immunity. The straight milk can really make you ill, causing high fever and a very upset stomach. Do not drink the milk. You can safely eat anything else the peasants may offer you, especially their baked goods, cheese products and excellent poultry. If you are invited to eat, do not offer to pay. However, expect to be approached to sell some dollars. Do it and don't worry if you get a little less than the true black market value. Peasants are, were, and in all likelihood will continue to be very shrewd.

CHAPTER EIGHT

Krakow: The City of Kings, Prelates and Learning

If this is your first trip to Poland, or even a return trip, you have to go to Krakow. The city is actually one thousand years old and was the capital of Poland from the 11th to the end of the 16th century. From the 15th to the 16th century it was one of the great centers of political power of Europe. In practical terms, this meant that the Polish kings attracted superb architects, painters, scholars, theologians, actors and poets. Powerful kings act like a magnet pulling the rich and the eager to settle in their orbit and build palaces, fund libraries, museums, support the arts and create the gloss, the patina, of an important city.

The presence of a king, his retinue and the aristocracy requires an appropriate infrastructure and demands a vigorous service industry, from cobblers to dressmakers, from gardeners to wine merchants. All of those came to Krakow and gave it the color, the vivaciousness, the pride that time and adversity have not erased. The inner city, dominated by the Wawel Castle, is elegant, a jewel of urban aesthetics. Not unlike the heart of Paris, Krakow's heart can only be seen by walking through it, enjoying its parks, the banks of the Vistula, and visiting the Jagiellonian University which was established in 1364 as the Krakow Academy. Since it gained its luster under the Jagiellonian kings it was informally called the Jagiellonian University. Today that is its official name. Among its many brilliant graduates, the best known is still Copernicus.

Usually American tourists, regardless of their level of education, have a problem with developing an appreciation for history and really do not know how to look at a city in an historical perspective. The U.S. is only two hundred years old and, even if we include the pilgrims our history, has yet to reach the fourth-century mark. We are only now beginning to preserve historical landmarks. Our economic and demographic imperatives demand that we destroy in order to expand. That was true of Krakow when it was only three hundred years old and that was seven hundred years ago. But since then the citizens of Krakow have defended the historical and aesthetic integrity of their city. They did it successfully until Stalinism sneaked in to build a huge steel mill, Nowa Huta, which employs about 40,000 workers and produces steel for which there is no market and for which the iron ore is delivered from the distant Urals where the Soviet iron ore deposits are located. The pollution caused by Nowa Huta could well destroy the beauty of Krakow, which no army in recent times has succeeded in doing. There is a fund to clean up the pollution emitted by Nowa Huta and to prevent the further deterioration of Krakow. The protection of the environment is the second priority of Poland; feeding its people is the first.

To describe the artistic and cultural centers of the city would require writing a huge tome which you would not have the time to read and which frankly would serve no purpose. You are in Krakow, there are guides, see it for yourself, and send postcards to your friends.

Krakow, however, has a few sights that we do want to talk about in a somewhat different context. These are the covered mall, officially identified as the Sukiennice (pronounced "Sookenitze") Clothiers Market, Wierzynek (pronounced "Vyezhinek"), the best restaurant in all of Poland and probably one of the best in Central Europe, the Marian Church (the Basilica of the Blessed Virgin Mary), one of Poland's most important shrines, and the Wavel (pronounced Vavel) Castle, which with its cathedral is regarded by most Poles as the spiritual center of the country.

Pope John Paul II, when he was still the Cardinal of Krakow, said in an introduction to a little book describing the Wawel Cathedral: ". . . and so he who enters this Cathedral, even as a chance pilgrim, must linger before this grandeur. The whole of our great thousand-year-old tradition, Christian and Polish at the same time, emerges as living reality in Wawel Cathedral. Historical tradition—these words seem to sound of the past, to speak of what is dead but yet remains in our memory. Meanwhile, tradition is that which was great and truly good, and so deserves to live on. Tradition is what gives birth to new life." The handsome little guide was first published in 1976. The copy from which the quotation was taken comes from a second printing which appeared in June 1981.

At a time when Poles lived under martial law, Solidarity was an underground organization, and its leader Lech Walesa was declared to be a non-person. Students who continued to defy the regime openly were brutally beaten, arrested and their leaders interned. What Solidarity was all about, what the young people forcibly expressed, was the truth "that tradition is that which was great and truly good and so deserves to live on. Tradition gives birth to new life." When you visit Krakow in 1990 and thereafter, you will feel and see and experience the historical truth contained in Cardinal Wojtyla's words. Poland is about freedom and its tradition gave birth to a new life in which hopes and dreams have the chance of becoming the realities of the future.

The day-to-day monuments of this great tradition are in evidence in Krakow's old town and especially on and around the great market place. We did mention the Clothiers Market, which is today a typical shopping mall, except that it is a beautiful Renaissance building. The mall is now the center for the sale of all types of folk art produced mainly by the mountain folk who live within a hundred miles of Krakow and by regional peasant cooperatives. Most of the folk art of Poland is sold by a cooperative known as Cepelia. The artists and artisans who produce it deliver a cornucopia of products ranging from marvelously carved chess pieces to intricately carved wooden boxes, decorative plates, handwoven wall hangings and rugs. You can also discover beautifully carved statutes, paintings on glass and artistic paper cut-outs of peasant life scenes suitable for framing. We recommend leatherwork—from intricately designed moccasins, to handbags, gloves and embroidered sheepskin lined jackets.

Peasant women spend the long winter evenings embroidering blouses, skirts, and tablecloths. These are truly unique. The designs identify the region of origin, but show a sufficient variation of detail to be considered highly individualistic. Although they are made of pure linen, they are sturdy and colorfast. They'll require drycleaning and have to be ironed. All of these articles can be purchased for zlotys and can be exported.

The recommended procedure is that you walk through the mall, look around, and then decide what you want to buy. Don't hesitate to bargain. There is a shortage of wrapping paper in Poland, so you would be well advised to buy one of those shopping nets which you can not fail to notice as part of the equipment carried around by men and women everywhere in Poland. You might be tempted to buy the kerchiefs the local women wear. They are colorful and peasant women from different regions tie them around their heads in a somewhat different fashion. But don't bother buying them because most are imported from Chicago. We will have more to say later on the subject of shopping in Poland. Yes, there are bargains because the average income of a worker is about $50 per month, which means that objects which require a lot of labor are inexpensive. Moreover, the drastic changes in Poland's economy and the emergence of privately owned shops have caused massive displacement of workers and ex-bureaucrats who need work. It will not be surprising if Poland became the place to shop in Europe. Eventually these changes will improve the standard of living of all Poles and prices, wages, and the value of Poland's currency will all go up, but for the near future Poland will be a bargain hunter's paradise.

If you are tired from your shopping expedition, you should have lunch at Wierzynek. Be sure that your hotel makes a reservation for you! It is virtually impossible to get a table without one. If you haven't the occasion to lunch there, a dinner is suggested.

The story of Wierzynek is fascinating. In the mid-14th century there lived in Krakow a very wealthy merchant with the name Wierzynek, who was of German origin, like most merchants at that time. During his lifetime Krakow was the center of a summit meeting of three of Europe's most powerful kings. Wierzynek decided to throw a party for them and regale them with the best dishes the cuisine could provide. The party was a success and the restaurant was born.

Wierzynek has survived, unmolested, by the various occupants of Poland and has maintained its private enterprise status throughout the Stalinist and strict socialist period of post-war Poland when all other restaurants were run by the government. Wierzynek owns its own fisheries, raises and butchers its own meat, and all the vegetables come from their gardens. Like any first class restaurant, they have their own bakery and pastry shop. The service is polite, quick, efficient. The decor and the place settings of silver and crystal are worthy of admiration. Although the check will be in zlotys, it will be high, and you would do well to tip the maître d and the waiter in dollars.

There is no good Polish wine. Wierzynek will have an assortment of good Hungarian red wines (Egri Bikaver) and a limited selection of French white wines. However, Poland has excellent brandies and liquors and a very good local beer. The coffee and the pastries, and above all the ice cream's, are delicious. They are served in a manner of old Vienna, from which Krakow inherited most of its *gemutlichkeit,* roughly meaning gentility and good taste.

The last of the sights on which we want spend some time is the church, built in 1221, which assumed its current form in the mid-14th century. The first thing you will notice is that the two steeples are uneven. Legend has it that the builder of the shorter one fell off and died. To honor him the steeple was not finished. Around the completed one there is a walkway. It was manned by a trumpeter whose duty was to sound the alarm if an enemy army approached the defensive walls of Krakow, still in evidence today.

And very often enemy armies did approach because Krakow lies on a plain which extends from the Ural Mountains 2,000 miles to the east to the plains of Germany. Between Krakow and the Urals there is no hill higher than 300 feet. This vast plain was the perfect invasion route for the Golden Hordes of Genghis Khan and his followers. In the middle of the 14th century a contingent of Tartar light horse cavalry approached Krakow. The trumpeter sounded the alarm, but was pierced by an arrow before he could complete it. Krakow was saved, the trumpeter was killed. To commemorate his devotion, every day at noon every radio and television station broadcasts the alarm and breaks it at the precise moment the original trumpeter was killed. This unbroken tradition has become the fabric of Poland's life. People set their watches by it. Incidentally, there are to this day, two trumpeters on duty 24 hours a day every day.

Inside the church stands one of the most famous altars of Christendom. It is a triptych sculptured in wood and heavily gilded with gold leaf. The altar is the work of Wit Stwosz who worked on it from 1477 to 1488. The altar depicts the life of the Holy Family. Its detail and the precision of the carving of the life-size figures is exquisite. The altar is very heavy, yet is so finely balanced that the merest touch at the center unfolds its full splendor. The altar is one of the greatest art treasures of Poland. You can imagine the imposing figure of Karol Wojtyla delivering his sermons there when he was the cardinal of Krakow. He has an astounding voice and a great presence, now known to all because as Pope John Paul II, his pilgrimages lead him all over the world. There is an affinity between the magnificence of the work of Wit Stwosz and the great dignity of the Pope.

While monuments and palaces give Krakow its distinctive aesthetic cachet, the way to get the real feel of the city is to take a walk along the Royal Route, once traversed by kings and foreign dignitaries. The walk begins at the Florian Gate which, together with the powerful bastion known as the Barbakan and neighboring walls, formed a powerful defensive structure, difficult to capture. After the defeat of the Tartar hordes and the increase in power of the Polish kingdom, most of the fortifications protecting the center of the town and the castle were destroyed and replaced by a circular park—a park replacing the wall—a symbolic expression of a hope for peace that carries a very contemporary meaning.

The walk around the Planty is a promenade through the glory of Poland's history, combined with the pleasure of seeing age-old trees and smiling faces of young people. You will be able to rest on comfortable benches undisturbed by the noises of a modern city. It is a place to dream about an unredeemable past.

At this point we got tired and returned to the Holiday Inn for a light dinner and a good night's rest. We suggest you do the same because we want you to visit three museums in the morning and be ready to leave Krakow early in the afternoon.

You have been to the mall, the Sukiennice, and you did what all tourists love to do: you bought mementos of your trip. Today we will take you back to the Sukiennice and walk up to the second floor. It's a gallery of Polish paintings. The most remarkable for its size, content, and mastery is the painting by Jan Matejko (1838–1893), who was born and lived in Krakow. It depicts the Prussian homage to the King of Poland. In 1525, Albrecht Hohenzollern, ancestor of Kaiser

Willhelm II who got the U.S. into World War I, knelt before
Sigmund the Old, King of Poland, Grand Duke of Lithuania,
and swore fealty. The Duke of Prussia accepted the
Suzerainty of Poland. The last Grand Master of the once
awesome Teutonic Knights accepted the fact that the King of
Poland was his superior. The Prussian homage took place on
the very same square you traversed.

Perhaps this is the right time to tell you that you are in a
royal city, in a place which was the largest multi-national
kingdom on the European continent since the fall of the
Roman Empire. The kingdom's moment of glory was short-
lived, but the memory of this glory is ever present in the
consciousness of most Poles.

Close to this painting is another of Matejko's masterpieces.
It depicts the victory of the Poles under the leadership of
Tadeusz Kosciuszko over the forces of Imperial Russia in the
battle of Raclawice fought in 1794. It was to be Poland's last
victory for nearly a century and half. You have the good
fortune of being in Krakow when Poland is again victorious.
This time it won a greater battle, a battle against enslavement
of its soul, against a constant degradation of its dignity by a
tyrannical system which will forever be known by the name
of the second greatest criminal of our century: Joseph Stalin.
There is an irony, a tragic irony in this tale. Lenin and Stalin
were in Krakow in 1906–7, and on orders of Lenin, Stalin
wrote a pamphlet entitled "On the Nationality Question," in
which he argued for the right of national self-determination
under a communist regime.

The second museum is in the Czartoryski Palace. This family is nearly as old as the Polish Nation and contributed to
Poland's glory and culture more than most of its peers. In the
palace are two magnificent paintings, one by Leonardo Da
Vinci, *The Lady with the Ermine*, and one by Rembrandt, *Land-
scape Before a Storm*. The museum contains about 550 paintings
including those of Bellini, Giordano and a host of Flemish
painters.

The third museum is a surprise, a surprise because it is a
functioning part of the Jagiellonian University. Many of the
great universities have museums on their campuses, but we

don't know of one that is truly a museum. The heart of the Jagiellonian University is the Collegium Maius. It was restored to its original gothic magnificence in the years between 1949 and 1964. As you walk through the Collegium, the Aula (Assembly Hall) and the Common Room, there are no single objects to point out. It is the integration of styles, artistry and mundane objects of yesteryear which create an ambiance that gives truth to the saying carved above a Renaissance portal: "Wisdom is greater than strength." Perhaps when we are out of our own dark ages, that saying will become the human reality.

Krakow, like Rome and Paris, has to be visited a few times before all of its beauty, diversity and sheer joy of living can be fully appreciated. All of us must do all we can do preserve that city.

The region around Krakow is beautiful and very interesting. The rolling hills, the Ojcow (pronounced "Oytzov") National Park, and the colorful farms are delightful to view. The park offers unusual sights: rock formations fascinating in form and deep canyons carved through the ages by two rivulets.

One of the most unique sights to be found anywhere in Europe is the Wieliczka (pronounced "Vyelichka") Salt Mine. It has been in continuous operation since 1290. Tourists can visit its deep shafts and observe a sight that is truly breathtaking, something which cannot be compared to any monument. Deep in the bowels of the mine is an altar to the Virgin Mary, hewn out of crystallized rock salt. When the long tapered candles burn, their reflection in the crystal create the impression of a chapel placed within a gigantic diamond. This altar, so deep in the soil of Poland, is an apt metaphor for the depth of faith animating the simple people of that land. Catholicism is the strong root of the Polish nation.

The salt mines of Wieliczka have produced millions of tons of salt in the long span of their existence. Fortunately the mines have their own museum which traces the story of the evolution of mining equipment. For some unknown reason there appears to be a health benefit from visiting the mines. There is some evidence that people visiting them experience a lasting relief from asthma. The mine has a perfect record of safety and tourists need have no fear descending into the shafts.

A little more than a one-hour drive from Krakow is Poland's most famous shrine, The Monastery of Jasna ("Yasna") Gora, which lies within the city limits of Czestochowa. The monastery contains the image of the Black Madonna. This icon of the Virgin Mary, painted in Byzantine style, was blackened by the smoke of artillery fire when it was carried on the ramparts of the monastery, besieged by Swedish armies in 1655. The Swedes, who had inundated all of Poland, were defeated by the defenders of Jasna Gora and the intervention of the Virgin Mary was credited with the victory. Shortly, thereafter, the Swedes retreated from Poland.

Every year on the Fete of the Assumption hundreds of thousands of pilgrims gather on the slopes leading up to the monastery (cared for by Pauline brothers) to pray, ask forgiveness and express their hope for a better future for themselves and their country. When John Paul II visited Poland in 1983, over a million people came to Jasna Gora.

The image of the Virgin is unveiled twice a day by devoted Pauline brothers entrusted with that task. The altar surrounding the icon is a repository for gifts from the faithful. They range from a humble offering to exquisite jewelry, and now the altar is adorned by a six-foot golden longstemmed American rose, a gift from John Paul.

It is possible that you might get to see the book of visitors who were asked to sign their names. For Americans there is one poignantly touching page. On top is the signature of John F. Kennedy, followed by the signature of Robert, Teddy, and Eunice and her husband Sargent Shriver. The last two came to Poland with their sons during the pope's visit. It is ironic that the book also has Hitler's signature. Every human person can ask the Virgin for grace, regardless of the sins committed.

It appears to be quite certain that Germany will be unified and the Poles are justifiably concerned that the Germans will raise the question of Poland's western frontiers which include lands that had previously belonged to the Third Reich. The Poles are quite aware that there are powerful interests currently in Germany that would like to regain these lands. It is appropriate, therefore, that we tell you about a ceremony that took place at Jasna Gora in the summer of 1985.

We have the pleasure of knowing Bishop Kazimierz Majdanski, a concentration camp martyr whose diocese includes the port city of Szczecin (Stettin) which belonged to Germany and is now part of Poland. The bishop asked us to come to Jasna Gora for a midnight mass. He did not tell us why. We arrived at about 11 PM and were escorted into the monastery by a young priest. He took us to the presbytery and motioned us to sit down in chairs provided for us. We were embarrassed because the chairs were on the left side of the altar, very close to Bishop Majdanski's place. The church was filled with mostly young people whose faces showed that they were tired, and their clothing indicated that they had come from afar. In fact they did. They were pilgrims who walked from Bishop Majdanski's diocese on the Baltic Sea to Jasna Gora, a distance of more than 500 miles. The purpose of their pilgrimage was to place the Recovered Lands of Poland under the protection of the Virgin Mary Queen of Poland. We have never in our lives considered faith to be a tangible force. But looking at these pilgrims and listening to their prayers, we felt the actual power generated by their faith. Tired as they were, their voices grew stronger as they prayed and sang the hymns. The Bishop's homily was reassuring, supportive, and loving, but not misleading. He told his congregation that their prayers are indeed needed and the protection of the Holy Queen of Poland asked for, to assure that their homes, their lands, their lives will remain within the domain of the crowned white eagle of Poland. The bishop blessed them and turned toward us and blessed us. We are not Catholics, yet grateful, and we joined the pilgrims in their prayers.

Also within the reach of Krakow are the concentration camps of Auschvitz-Birkenau. Their existence has no place in a book devoted to tourism. Take a day off from being a tourist to pay homage to martyrs, but do not make that day part of your itinerary. One does not visit the grave of a butchered father or brother-human inbetween lunch and dinner.

CHAPTER NINE

The Mountains, the Forests and Their Fiercely Independent People

About a hundred miles due south of Krakow, you enter Poland's beautiful mountain range. The range known in this area as the Tatra Mountains has many names. Actually the Tatra Mountains are a part of the Carpathian Mountain range, which in turn is a section of a mountain range that reaches all the way across southern Europe to Pakistan. On many of the

wooden carvings of Polish mountaineers, you are likely to
find an emblem resembling the swastika in reverse. The emblem is a design present in folkloric carvings also in Pakistan.
Perhaps this is a coincidence, but more likely it is one of those
mysterious continuities of history documenting the migration
of peoples.

The Tatra Mountains are the favorite playground of Poland.
The tourist center is Zakopane. Except for a few beautiful
villas and some shops featuring the richly embroidered
mountaineer festival costumes, Zakopane itself is an ugly
city. The only hotel worth staying in, the Kasprowy, is slightly
outside of Zakopane. It is new, luxurious, and its balconies
provide a panorama of the mountains. The tallest are the
Kasprowy and the Rysy which reach heights of 2500 meters.
Only Alpine climbers have the skill to make it to the top of
those. For others who do not have these skills there is a cable
car to the top of the Kasprowy (about 2000 meters, 6500 feet
high) from which you can see on a clear day the entire Tatra
range. The Kasprowy has been named after the poet Jan
Kasprowicz who resided in Zakopane. It would take a poet to
describe the beauty of the view from the Kasprowy.

Throughout this guide we have been recommending that
you stay only in first class hotels. Now it's time for an exception. Before you leave Krakow, try to make an arrangement
through the concierge in your hotel, or if you took our advice
and hired a driver, enlist his help, to find a place for you to
stay in one of the many mountaineer houses that offer rooms
to rent. For a moment, we will skip the description of the
marvelous wooden architecture of the homes and entice you
to sleep, for once in your life, on a mattress filled with fragrant
hay with your head resting on huge, soft down-filled pillows,
and be covered by a mountainous comforter filled with feathers. All of the bedding in these rooms is covered with homespun, embroidered linen. The walls are wide wooden planks
made air tight by intricately woven flax and straw. The aroma
of the room rivals the appealing, sense-overpowering mountain air.

The homes have electricity, 220 volts. You should have an
immersion heater with you to boil water if you have to have

your coffee the first thing in the morning. Chances are that in your room you will have a wash basin and a pitcher which the landlady will fill with water. The simple furnishings will fill you with envy. The window curtains will be snow white and embroidered with lace. Wooden chairs, nicely and simply carved, will surprise you by their comfort and the support they provide your back. The wooden table is likely to be covered with a plastic table cloth. (An excusable lapse from the generally prevailing good taste). Spills wipe off easily and after all you will be in the room for just a night or two.

Chances are that you will have to use an outhouse. It's not as uncomfortable as you imagine, and compared to some of the bathrooms you might encounter in the area hotels, you may wish you had opted for the outhouse earlier.

Knowing the sense of hospitality of the mountain people, you will be invited to breakfast—and that will be a feast. They smoke their own sausage which usually is a delightful mix of veal and pork. You will also experience the taste of real peasant bread. Long after you've left that home you will remember the taste of that bread. Not even Bloomingdales gourmet deli has anything approaching it in either taste or in the crispness of the crust. With the sausage you will be served two kinds of cheeses, goat cheese, which is pungent and on the sharp side, or a local cheese, cone-shaped and available only in the Tatra region. A lot of people really like it. For our tastes, it was a little too dry. The other breakfast delicacies are incredibly flavorful mountain honey, explainable by the aroma of the flowers from which the bees collected their nectar. Usually there will also be some sweets. One of them is the babka (a pound cake), found throughout Poland, but in the mountains it has an especially delicate flavor.

You will eat with the family in the kitchen. The food is cooked on an old-fashioned woodburning stove covered with a table-sized iron plate. The fire is laid out in a way to provide the cooking surface with different temperatures. The center will be the hottest and used for boiling water, the rims will be cooler, good for simmering soups. The sides of the oven are tiled as is the attached baking and roasting area. This section towers above the plate. It serves three purposes; to bake bread, make roasts, and to heat the kitchen in the winter. Actually the double windows of the huts and the very tight construction allow the kitchen oven to heat the house. The sleeping quarters are cool, but that is healthy and under the down-filled covers you are quite cozy.

In nearly every room there will be a crucifix and frequently you will find an inexpensive print of Jesus with the exposed heart.

The mountain people are very status conscious and proud. This becomes very evident at weddings, first communions and important holidays. The jewelry worn by the women are the traditional red corals and quite frequently twenty dollar gold pieces. The men proudly referring to themselves as *gorale* (pronounced goorale), as opposed to peasants, wear magnificently embroidered heavy woolen pants and drape equally colorful capes around their shoulders. Many of these men and fewer women either worked in the United States or have relatives there, which makes it possible for them to own more than just one acre of land and perhaps even possible to build another house that eventually will become the home for one of their children. Sometimes they will even purchase farm implements.

Naturally someone returning from America will bring a lot of gifts: sweaters, sneakers, jeans, blouses with gold threads, a portable radio, and a few twenty dollar gold pieces. They are destined for the wife and as dowries for daughters. These days he may even buy a car and use it as a local taxi.

Despite this wealth, the family's life style will not change. Every morning the oldest son or daughter will take the cows to pasture, the man will work in the field and the woman will tend to the hens and geese, help milk the cows, cook and bake and gossip with her neighbors. Looking in from the outside, you would never guess they are well off, or even that they know that this is the 20th century. They do it on purpose. If they changed visibly, the authorities would bother them, force them to change their way of life, and generally interfere. As it is, due to their remote location from the capital of whatever power or system happens to rule Poland, they are left alone. They were, they are, and they will remain, strictly private enterprises. They miss the Jews who used to live in the market towns. They miss the credit they could get, they miss the important news of the world. And many of them helped Polish Jews and non-Jews escape to Hungary during WW II, where they were safe at least for a while.

The Nazis, for example, tried to convince them that they are not Poles but Goralenvolk, a special Aryan species. The mountaineers told them to "fly a kite." When pressed, the men often went up into the mountains, which they know like the proverbial backs of their hands, and disappeared. The Nazis gave up. Without making a comparison, so did the communists.

The only constant among the villagers is the Church, and the real authority is the village priest who educates their children, the parish priest who sees to it that they are good Catholics, and the bishop who is the revered authority.

Hopefully you will be in one of these villages on a Sunday when all the inhabitants are dressed in their costumes. You will witness an explosion of color, magnificent embroidery and after the Mass, boisterous fun. Their atonal singing will cause even a devotee of punk rock to stuff his ears with cotton. You would miss all that if you opted for the luxury of the Kasprowy, but you could still admire the wooden architecture of the villages, visit a magnificent wooden church and take breathtaking excursions into the mountains.

We always ask you to go for a walk. Ask your driver to take you to the Dolina Chocholowska ("Hoholovska"), one of the favorites of the Pope, who loves those mountains and who knows them well. A dolina is a flat area between mountain peaks, surrounded by huge pine trees and usually used for sheep grazing. This particular dolina is so peaceful and somehow so well placed, it creates an enchantment words cannot portray. Walk in the woods, over beds of pine needles rendered soft by rain and age. Listen to the birds, the rustling of the trees, and catch a glimpse of the sky and the mountain tops. The place defies time, history, personal worries, and invites a free flow of dreams and imagination.

The local tourist office (PTTK) will tell you what you must see, and for once they will be right.

CHAPTER TEN

Along the Mountain Range to the Core of Peasant Country

The southern section of Poland was occupied for over a century by the Austrio-Hungarian Empire. The Empire was liberal and tolerant. Toward the end of the 19th century Polish politicians played leading roles in the governance of the Empire, thus Polish culture flourished. Unfortunately the Empire was very late in joining the industrial revolution and most of its provinces were poor, especially the Polish province of Galicia. The only real wealth was distributed among a handful of large land owners and a few merchants, most of them

Jewish. However, the general population included hundreds
of thousands of Jews, living a miserable existence. The peasants in that area of Poland were the only segment of the
population that benefited from the post-WWII socialist regime. They were allowed to keep their land, given an opportunity to acquire more and the government gave them substantial subsidies to grow food and raise poultry. Just to give
you an example: an egg for which a city dweller used to pay 2
zlotys cost the government about 5 zlotys. The worst off were
and are actually the city dwellers and the workers, despite the
fact that the communist government allocated an enormous
percentage of its budget for a variety of social services and
subsidies. Most were mismanaged by a bloated bureaucracy,
but some still delivered. The new Polish government, freed of
the yoke of communist dogmatic approaches to economic
management is dismantling this bureaucracy and creating a
market-oriented economy. The cost of this restructuring will
be born primarily by city dwellers and workers. They will
have to pay for the inefficiencies and thievery by a regime that
was in power for about 45 years. Whole segments of Polish
industry will have to be either abandoned or turned into
profitable enterprises. Important projects like apartment
building, modernization of the communication system and
above all the saving of the environment (cleaning Poland's
water supply, purifying the air, and clearing the soil from the
impurities deposited by industry) will have to receive high
priorities. And while this is going on, many workers, secre-
taries and administrators will be unemployed. The costs of all
these changes will consume enormous sums and there will be
little left for a social safety net. It is not because the Solidarity
government is heartless, but because even with Western financial help, there will not be enough money to take care of
all the needs of the Polish population. If there ever was a need
for Poles living and earning in the West to help Poland's
people, now is the time. We know that you know, but the
problems are so enormous and the help so urgently needed
that we believe that we are justified in digressing from the
basic purpose of this book.

All of this, however, does not change the fact that the one

hard working and relatively independent sector of the Polish society is the peasants. That situation is not likely to change soon.

As a peasant woman told us, "If the government raises butter prices, or rations butter, we can make our own." And they do. It's quite a sight to see a family and friends sitting in the kitchen taking turns churning milk into butter. The conversation is lively and the vodka bottle is passed around. Many peasants have a traditional way of drinking, using only one shot glass which a number of people share. This imposes a fast-paced consumption. Your neighbor in the circle will fill the glass, drink to your good health, then refill it, and pass it on to you. You'll drink to your neighbor's health—it's always consumed in one gulp—fill it and pass it on. You would be amazed how quickly a bottle is emptied and just when you are ready to sigh in relief, a peasant companion in the butter churning circle will pull another bottle from his deep pant's pocket, and the circle starts all over. There is no doubt that when they find out an American is in their village, you will be invited. You should do it once. You can sleep the effects off in any convenient haystack. Inbetween gulps you eat the excellent bread and pickles or herring if it is available.

Poland used to be one of the largest herring exporters in Europe. Now, because of the pollution of the Baltic, Poland has to import herring from Iceland. Be this as it may, peasant gatherings are still quite a party during which all the affairs of the world get settled. We tried the vodka custom when we returned to New York. It worked well. As a matter of fact we too had quite a party.

A Galician hamlet consists of about 200 homesteads. Most of them are constructed of wood and have thatched roofs. But the homes of those who have been to America have brick walls and a lot of plastic gadgets in the kitchen. You can be certain to be invited if you first pay a visit to the local priest, or if you let it be known that you want to trade a pair of jeans, for example. It does not matter if they are a little worn, and, of course, dollars are always welcome.

Your trip from Zakopane to your eventual destination at the fortress town of Przemysl ("Pshemisl") should take a few hours, but we hope you are able take a couple of days. We know that tourist days are precious and there is a lot left to see, but there is so much beauty in that part of Poland that it would be a pity to miss it. In a very personal way I am prejudiced because I was born in that part of Poland and have the fondest memories of a very sunny and fun-filled childhood. So, if you go off the main road, you will have the chance to visit a number of Poland's fabulous spas, usually located on the banks of small rivers rushing down from the mountains. The water is refreshingly cold, excellent to drink, affords fishing, and the air is among the purest in the world. The pervasive pollution fortunately did not ruin this part of Poland. The crown jewel of the resorts is Krynica (Krynitsa). The climate is mild, the waters have all the attributes of the proverbial snake oil, guaranteed to cure most digestive disorders.

In fact there are magnificent parks and gently sloping woods to walk in. Most of Poland's really well equipped rest homes are in Krynica, so also is the Patria, an elegant pre-war hotel built by Jan Kiepura, world famous tenor who in the thirties performed in the world's most prestigious opera houses from the Scala of Milan to New York's Metropolitan. The clientele has changed, but the hotel is still first rate. You might want to spend a night there, but be sure you have a reservation.

As a matter of fact, if you choose to travel at a leisurely pace through the route along the foothills of southern Poland, you are bound to go through many county seats. The lowest branch of the administrative structure of Poland is known as the *Powiat* ("poviat") and is located in a small town of usually not more than 10,000 inhabitants. Most of these small towns have been spared the destruction of both world wars. Consequently, when you visit them you will gain a deep insight into the daily lives of the largest segment of the Polish population. The church in the powiat town will be larger than the churches in the small villages. Usually the powiat church will be headed by a monsignor, a priest higher in the ecclesiastical rank than the village priest, and usually the most powerful and influential personage in the town. Neither the extinct, former Communist regime, nor the present Solidarity regime would dare to trifle with the monsignor.

We have to digress here to tell you a story which reveals how things were done in Poland and probably will continue to be done out of sight of Warsaw.

We were invited to participate in a local harvest festival and for some reason the chairman of the Council of State, at that time an honorific position roughly equivalent to the president of a country, decided to visit that particular ceremony. He came with his entourage of dignitaries, was greeted by the local party leader (who was also the mayor of the town), the monsignor, the head of the school distrist, and other local personalities. After the official part of the ceremony ended, the chairman, the mayor, the school administrator and the monsignor engaged in a lively discussion. It seems that the roof of the local school house had developed so many leaks that it had to be replaced, but despite many petitions to the Ministry of Education, the local administrator could not get the necessary allocation of tin plates to make a new roof for the school. He proceeded to ask the chairman to intervene on behalf of the children of the powiat and get the new roof. The chairman, former university professor, said that he really sympathized with the administrator's problem and pointedly gazing at the shiny new roof of the church continued what he wanted to say: "Why are you asking me? Look at the shiny new roof of your church. You know whom to ask when you need to get things done and done well." And while he was saying this he turned toward the monsignor who grinned like a satisfied Cheshire cat. In Poland, since forever, if you needed something done in a hurry, you went either to the monsignor or the rabbi, while they were around.

Incidentally, we happened to go back to that village a year later and the school did have a new roof. Since we knew the monsignor, we asked him how the school happened to get a new roof. He told us: "It seems that the Cardinal Archbishop of Krakow—at that time Karol Wojtyla—decided to make a visitation to the Powiat shortly before the start of the new school year, following the ceremony we participated in. Now, the government in Warsaw really did not want to hear a sermon on the subject of how it neglects the educational needs of the children by making them go to schools with leaking roofs. Rather than run the risk of a confrontation with the powerful and outspoken cardinal, it was far more expeditious to give the school not only a new roof, but also new gym equipment." So ends our short lesson in Polish politics.

The real reason we recommend that you stay in a powiat town for a couple of hours is to see the drabness, the monotony which is interrupted only once a week by a market day. In the center of the town you will find a large empty square bordered by a few shops with meager assortments of farm supplies, a number of quasi-restaurants which actually serve poor quality sausage and cheap vodka, and perhaps you will also see a stationery store with a poor selection of school supplies. On a market day, however, the square is full of noise, milling throngs from the entire powiat, and filled with stalls selling agricultural products, food and implements, but mostly trading cows and work horses. Above all, you will see clothes, folk art, and plastic . . . well, "things."

The selling of animals is a man's job, but all the rest of the trading is done by middle-aged and elderly women in colorful kerchiefs and the ever present coral beads. Legend has it that these beads have the magic of bringing good luck in the form of many, healthy children, preferably boys. (There may be truth to the legend. Poland's population grew from less than 28 million after the war to 38 million today.)

You will be surprised and amused by the prominently displayed labels on the clothes that are being traded. For a moment you might think that you have walked into an American discount house. As a matter of fact, everything from socks to underwear to braziers, ball point pens to small radios will be American.

If you listen in on the "horse trading" and have the patience to wait until the transaction is completed, a fact marked by a handshake and a deep gulp of vodka straight from the bottle, you will notice hundred dollar bills changing hands between the buyer and the seller. Nothing of real value, like land, a house, and an apartment, is sold for zlotys; private business is done in dollars. When we saw it, this was illegal. Today the zloty is convertible within the country and all dollar (or any Western currency) transactions are legal. The markets are weekly affairs usually held on a Wednesday or Thursday.

The two items we suggest you buy at the markets are fur caps and short fur-lined (sheep skin) coats. If you happen to be very lucky, you might find homespun linen shirts and tablecloths. Grab them. They are wonderful. The tablecloth will be hand embroidered.

Traveling along secondary roads in the shadows of the mountain range, known in this area as the Carpathians, will bring you to our favorite area of Poland. This is the Bieszczady ("Beskedees") region. It is the wildest, least populated and without doubt the most attractive tourist area of Poland. The government has been trying to develop it, but fortunately has not as yet succeeded.

This part of Poland borders on the Soviet Union. Prior to 1939, it was close to the center of southern Poland. Its inhabitants are identified as the Huculs ("Hootzools"). They are every bit as colorful as the mountaineers, but are not as hospitable and certainly not as open. Their native costumes are outstanding and quite different in artistic detail from those of Poland's other mountaineers. They speak in their own particular dialect and have a negative attitude towards Poles in general and foreigners in particular. But they like the cash income tourism provides. It probably is the only cash income they have. Their economy is still based primarily on barter.

Your driver can find the small town of Lesko, which is the beginning of the Bieszczady loop. The forests are noteworthy for their rich foliage and wild game, ranging from brown bears to wolves and lynx deer. The woods are also quite full of snakes. If you venture in for a walk, have a guide and wear high leather boots. Our advice is to look at the scenery from the safety of your car, but do visit the villages and the Greek Orthodox wooden churches with some of the most interesting icons to be found outside of Russia.

We recommended that you stay overnight in Przemysl,

rather than the better known Rzeszow, which you can visit together with its environs on your leisurely way back to Warsaw. Przemysl has so much history and is so interesting. There is an adequate Orbis Hotel for your night's rest.

Przemysl and the nearby town of Jaroslaw are an architectural mixture of Eastern and Western Europe. Both, about a thousand years old, owe their existence to their position astride the San River, one of the most important trade routes linking the rich principality of Kiev with the Baltic Sea, and thus one of the main trade routes of medieval Europe. The areas around both towns, as well as of Lublin, were the centers of Jewish settlements and world famous Jewish schools of learning (yeshivas). Nothing is left of these settlements, but it is still possible to recognize a Jewish house. It is usually two stories high. On the ground floor you will notice a large window clearly used to display the merchandise available in the store in front. To the left of the window there will be a wide doorway closed by a single wooden gate, reaching from the floor to the arched ceiling. The doorway was wide enough to accommodate a heavily laden cart capable of transporting kegs of wine, bolts of cloth and the other paraphernalia of the traditional Jewish trading businesses. Both towns feature Poland's outstanding Renaissance architecture. Both of them housed families of very wealthy merchants who could afford ornate homes and since most Polish towns had a vigorous self-governing structure, they competed in creating imposing town halls and market squares. Przemysl, the larger of the two towns, declined during the 17th and 18th centuries. But in the mid-19th century, the Austrian Empire decided to fortify the city and change it into a defense bastion. During World War I, the Imperial Russian armies bombarded Przemysl and a lot of its historic beauty was destroyed. However the Gothic and Baroque churches survived, as did most of town's center.

You owe it to yourself to see how Poland's magnates lived on their lands. You saw some of their palaces in Warsaw and Krakow, but they pale into insignificance compared to their ancestral estates. Close to Przemysl is Krasiczyn (Cracitchyn),

1 The Old Town market square, Warsaw

2 The Grand Theatre and Opera House, Warsaw

3 The modern city centre, Warsaw

4 Wilanów, King Jan Sobieski's palace outside Warsaw

5 The Przybyła houses, Kazimierz Dolny

6 Baranów castle

7 The towers of Wawel cathedral, Cracow

8 St. Mary's church, Cracow

9 The Cloth Hall and Town Hall tower, Cracow market square

10 Jasna Góra monastery, Częstochowa

11 Pieskowa Skała castle seen from the road below

12 Pieskowa Skała courtyard

13 Folk festival at Nowy Sącz

14 Mount Giewont in the Tatra range

15 Hill-farming in southern Poland

16 Wrocław University

17 Lądek Zdrój in the Kłodzka Valley

18 Old market square and Town hall, Poznań

19 Country inn, Poznań province

20 Hunting at Biały Bór, Koszalin province

21 The beach at Cetniewo

22 The Artus mansion, Gdańsk

23 Malbork castle

24 Bison, Białowieża forest

25 Lake Białe, near Augustów

26 Pre-Christian stone statue from Barciany, now in the courtyard of Olsztyn castle

the residence of the Krasicki family, and a little further is Lancut, the home of the Potockis, but actually owned by the Lanckoronskis. All three of those names appear at least once in every chapter of Poland's history. Most of their palaces were built by Italian architects who came to Poland with Queen Bona, wife of Sigmund Jagiello. Queen Bona was the daughter of the Condotierri Sforza, conqueror of Milan, who proclaimed himself to be a duke. Bona Sforza was very intelligent and had a keen taste for beauty. As her retinue, she brought architects, gardeners, painters, sculptors, scholars and physicians to Poland. Following Queen Bona's example, the magnate families brought their exponents of the Italian Renaissance to build their residences. The magnate families competed with the royal court in the elegance and opulence of their family palaces. You have to visit them to feel the grandeur of their wealth, stature and pride.

If you have only two weeks, they are nearly up and you should start your trip back to Warsaw. Take your time to visit Rzeszow, Lublin, and a jewel of a small town, Kazimierz Dolny (Kazimis Dolny). It's as charming a town as you can find anywhere in Europe. There is also Zamosc, built by the Zamoyski family as a typical Italian Renaissance town. It is incredible to find it in the middle of Poland, perfectly preserved and perhaps possessing more architectural integrity than most Italian towns dating from 1578. The entire area around Lublin is one huge Renaissance museum, each town sufficiently different to warrant a glance; the distances between them are insignificant and can be covered in a two-day trip. Both Lublin and Rzeszow have well furnished Orbis hotels. Lublin is now gaining international recognition as the town in which the Catholic University of Poland is located and where Karol Wojtyla taught philosophy and theology. His students are today leading intellects in Catholic centers throughout the world.

Traveling slowly through rich fields and forests, you soon reach the outskirts of Warsaw. You saw some of Poland, but there is so much more left to see. Actually, you should have applied for a three-week visa. If you have to leave early, the zlotys you have left will be refunded to you in dollars at the official, privately owned currency exchanges. But you can always extend your visa. The Orbis office at your hotel in Warsaw will tell you how to do it. It will take you about one hour. If you can afford the time, we suggest you extend your stay.

CHAPTER ELEVEN

Gniezno: The Cradle of Polish Catholicism

After your arduous trip through southern Poland, you should take a day's rest in Warsaw, then begin an exploration of the northern part of Poland by an excursion to the birthplace of Poland's Catholicism.

Roman Catholicism became Poland's official religion in stages beginning in 966. In practical terms, this meant that Poland's first king, Mieszko I ("Mieshko"), converted to Christianity, but most of the remaining inhabitants of Poland, actually a host of Slavic tribes, continued their pagan practices until 1226, when all these tribes converted to Roman Catholicism. Mieszko's first wife died and he subsequently married a nun named Oda. It is fascinating that we know all these tidbits about the birth of Catholicism in Poland from the writings of Ibrahim-Ibn-Jacub, presumably a Jewish trader, who somehow found his way to Gniezno, probably on his way to the Baltic to purchase some amber. A few years later when Polish kings, specifically Mieszko II, began to mint their own currency, they engraved in Hebrew letters the word "shalom," meaning "peace" on the obverse side of the first silver coin. The history of the Poles and the Jews is intertwined by ten centuries of common experiences which the creation of the State of Israel cannot obliterate.

The importance of Gniezno is that it was the first bishopric in Poland. When the Apostolic Universal Roman Catholic Church decided to establish a new diocese, it not only converted a nation to a faith, but it also extended the territory under the protectorate of the Holy Roman Empire of the German Nation. In the 10th century, the pope as the Pontifex Maximus, the title of the Roman Ceasars, recognized Germany as the rightful inheritor of the secular strength of the Roman Empire.

Thus Mieszko's conversion marks the beginning of two themes which remained constant throughout Poland's secular history. It placed Poland within the sphere of Roman, meaning Western civilization, and it placed Poland in a subservient relationship to the German emperor and thus laid the foundations for a struggle that was to continue for ten centuries.

In a book devoted to tourism, there is no room to trace the turbulent history of Catholicism in Poland and the convoluted relationship between the Church in Poland and the popes residing in the distant Vatican. However, you are now about to enter the part of Poland which was an area for centuries of brutal and bloody strife between Poles and Crusaders, supported and protected by a number of popes. The Crusaders, having failed in their primary mission to liberate the Holy Land, spent their energies plundering many areas of Europe, northern Poland being among them. It was the Crusaders who made Prussia into a military camp and in 1410, when they were finally defeated by the Poles in the battle of Grunwald, moved across the Baltic and settled in provinces known as Livonia and Curland. Both of these provinces were occupied for a time by Poland, subsequently conquered by the Swedes, and eventually ended under the rule of the Imperial Russian family. Today they are known as Estonia and Latvia, names resurrected from their distant, pagan past.

This marginal note is important because you constantly hear that the Polish people are 95 percent Catholic. The statistics are correct, but they do not reflect the reality of the relationship of Polish Catholics with the Holy See.

Gniezno is only about an hour's drive from Warsaw and is to this day the official administrative center of Poland's Catholic Church and the residence of the Cardinal Primate of Poland. The title "primus" has an interesting history. Whenever a king was to be elected, the cardinal primus was the effective ruler of Poland during the interregnum, which usually was a bit of time. The actual residence of the primus was a magnificent palace in Warsaw. Today he occupies somewhat more modest quarters on Miodowa Street in Warsaw, a short walking distance from the Royal Palace.

The Catholicism of the Polish peasants is simple, sometimes crude, and very little influenced by Rome, until most recently. Since the election of Karol Wojtyla to the throne of St. Peter, the Vatican semi-official publication "Osservatore Romano" appears in a Polish language version.

The Polish intellectuals and most of the Polish *szlachta* and nobility are basically secular and proclaim their adherence to Catholicism only on Sundays and holidays.

During the recent period of martial law, the Church offered a safe haven for Solidarity activists and engaged many of its resources augmented by the generosity of the pope to further the knowledge of real Polish history and culture, especially among the younger generation. Particularily deeply involved in these unparalled educational activities were the lower ranks of the Catholic official family. They perceived that the young people will carry the burden of reestablishing the continuity of the values that kept the Polish nation intact through the Hitler/Stalin era of ruthless suppression. These inexperienced and ill taught youth have to learn what actually made Poland's culture so vibrant and noteworthy. It can be stated without fear of exaggeration that without the Church assuming the role of educator, Poland's youth would have become disoriented and mentally incapable of assuming leadership roles. But the clergy also fought for freedom from the pulpit and paid for its involvement with their personal freedom and in one instance with their lives. The martyr of the Solidarity fight which broke the communist stranglehold on Poland was the magnificent human being, the gentle, kind, and always ready to serve Father Popieluszko, pastor of Warsaw's Church of Saint Stanislaw Kostka. He was murdered by members of Poland's People Militia who "acted on their own," without orders from their superiors. These activities accounted for the Church's popularity and the active participation of the masses at church services. John Paul II supported Solidarity (not so much the organization as its aims). By his power of persuasion and adroit political moves, John Paul II made it possible for tens of thousands of Poles to come on pilgrimages to Rome. Every Wednesday the Pope holds a public audience at St. Peters square. During the ten years (and more to come) of his pontificate, the Pope has held more than 500 such audiences and at every one there was a sizable contingent from Poland, frantically waving the banners which identified the region of Poland they represented. The Pope never fails to say a few encouraging words to them and reaches out to touch them and bless them. The pilgrims and their Pope share the joy of seeing each other. Actually John Paul's voice when he speaks in Polish retains the timbre and energy of a young man. Often he makes time to see a visitor from Poland, and time permitting gives private audiences for smaller groups.

By coincidence, we were in Rome, when Bishop Majdanski brought a hundred or more of his paritioners for such an audience. We saw them go in and come out inspired and rejuvenated. It is impossible for us to explain the impact of John Paul on his countrymen, and if we hadn't seen it we would not believe that one man, even a pope, can have such an impact. Because of him, there is a John Paul II Foundation in Rome which is equipped to house and feed hundreds of pilgrims, further their knowledge of Catholicism and of Polish culture. The long road of the Polish Pope began a thousand years ago in Gniezno.

While it is understandable that Polish pilgrims would go to Rome to see the Pope, they also go to enjoy the air of freedom and take in the sights of Rome, just like any tourist. But so harsh is life in Poland that many pilgrims are less interested in the Pope and show more concern in buying some of the material goods which are in demand back home. These pilgrimages are not cheap, but it is possible to get back the cost and even turn a profit.

While on the subject of the Pope, we want to tell you a story of what happened to one of America's "household" name families who came to Poland in 1983, during the Pope's second pilgrimage to his homeland. This outstanding Catholic American clan wanted to see John Paul in native surroundings. We got to Krakow on the very day the Pope conducted a solemn Mass of canonization of Maximilian Kolbe and consecrated the church located in Nowa Huta, not too far from the decrepit steel mill. The church is named after the saint who was a saint even in nontheological terms. He voluntarily took the place of a Dachau prisoner when the SS murder squad was in need of one more body to make their daily quota. Kolbe died in one of the ovens; the man he saved is alive to this day.

The family flew in from Warsaw by helicopter, which landed a very short distance from the Pope. We had excellent seats. It was a hard to describe scene. Not only were there more than half a million people from all over Poland, but also all the ambassadors and the rest of the diplomatic corps. The scene of thousands of officially banned Solidarity banners and signs created an atmosphere of a political convention. The slogan of the day was "They (the thugs of the secret police) can not beat us today because the Pope is here—we can say what we want." It was true. The police were out in force and had convoys of the dreaded screened wagons in which prisoners were transported. None of this escaped notice of the American family. The boys joined the protest march after the Mass and, although they did not speak Polish, they picked up the Polish way of pronouncing Solidarity, linked arms with others, and the American consul had a temper tantrum. To no effect.

When the Mass ended and the Pope left in his popemobile, the thousands of peasants all dressed in their most colorful costumes began to sing and dance. The Pope had brought with him the aroma of freedom which stayed in the air even after he left.

Our seats were close to a group of mountaineers. Suddenly one of the dancers spotted the American family and drew them into the circle of dancers. For a moment they were self conscious, but after a mountaineer woman placed her kerchief around the neck of the lady and a mountaineer man gave his colorful hat, the prominent American family threw themselves into the dance with a gusto and enthusiasm uncharacteristic of a sophisticated Washingtonian. The Pope, the Mass and that dance are the most outstanding memories they brought back with them. They had seen the palaces and cathedrals of the world, but only in Poland, for a brief moment, did they make contact with a small group expressing the joy of living proof that faith is necessary.

Visually, the Cathedral of Gniezno resembles in its Gothic style the cathedrals you encounter throughout Catholic Europe. The distinguishing characteristic of the Gniezno Cathedral is its bronze door whose twelve panels depict the life and martyrdom of Poland's first saint. His Church-given name is St. Adalbert; his Polish name is St. Wojciech. He was murdered by the Prussian tribes whom he tried to convert to Catholicism.

Standing in the shadows of the Gniezno Cathedral, you might want to reflect upon the fact that if that cathedral had an onion-shaped dome of a Greek Orthodox cathedral, Poland would have been the Westernmost exponent of the Byzantine Empire which adopted Greek Orthodoxy, broke with Rome, and created the civilization that permeated Russia. It shaped its history and thus would have shaped the history of Poland and, by extension, of all of Europe. The fact that you are standing under the Roman cross placed there a thousand years ago means that you are looking at a spot which marks a turning point in world history.

The culture and the values by which people live and through which they try to shape the kind of a society and government they desire are rooted in their beliefs, in their faith, and hence in their religion. Greek Orthodoxy converted millions of East Europeans to its tenets based on obedience, conformity, and cultural subservience. With perhaps one or two exceptions, the great Russian writers spent some time in Siberian exile. Had Greek Orthodoxy gained the upper hand in Poland, had Greek Orthodoxy built the Cathedral of Gniezno, Poland would have become only a name on a map, a very detailed map. It is Gniezno which made the Poles freedom fighters. This relatively small cathedral helped draw the line between the West and the East, between a Roman culture and a Byzantine culture.

CHAPTER TWELVE

Gdansk and the Beauty of the Baltic Sea

The Baltic Sea is the northern counterpart of the Mediterranean Sea. It links Poland with the Scandinavian countries, and through the narrows of Denmark, with the oceans of the world and its important trading centers. The most important port on the Baltic Sea is Gdansk, the city which lies at the estuary of the Vistula River, Poland's arterial highway of trade. The river is navigable and linked with a number of other rivers forms one of the most important trade routes from the East (for silk, spices, gems) to northern and western Europe. The link between the Black Sea and the Baltic was lucrative and vital to the well being of the old continent as long as Europe's principal trade was with the distant East. The fact that a powerful, stable kingdom controlled the shores of both seas offered a measure of security for traders and traveling merchants.

The change in the trading patterns of Europe which followed the discovery of the New World was one of the principal factors in the decline of many northern European port cities, including Gdansk. In time this process was reversed. The intervention of the steamship and the general integration of the world economy helped the renaissance of Gdansk. Today it is the home port of one of the world's largest shipping lines, and prior to the emergence of Korea as the major ship builder, Poland was an important center of that industry. The Gdansk shipyards, notably the Lenin Shipyard, gained international recognition as the birthplace of Solidarity.

Important as that event looms in the current consciousness of the world, Gdansk has a long distinguished and historically significant past. The Polish kings fought for centuries to control Gdansk and generally the southern ports of the Baltic from Szczecin, which lies at the mouth of the Oder River, to Gdansk and beyond. For a short period, toward the end of the 16th century, the Polish kingdom claimed control over the Gulf of Riga (today Latvia's territorial water). But the crown jewel of the southern Baltic coast was and remains Gdansk. Gdansk, Szczecin (Stettin) and provinces around it enjoyed relative peace from 1410 when the Polish armed forces defeated the Teutonic Knights until the outbreak of World War II. There were a few disturbing moments in the inbetween periods, but no major catastrophies. In the partitions of Poland, Gdansk became part of the Prussian kingdom, which changed the name of Gdansk to Danzig, and of Szczecin to Stettin.

At the conclusion of World War I, Gdansk was declared a free city, administered by a high commissionair appointed by the League of Nations. This compromise was necessary because Poland's access to the Baltic Sea separated East Prussia from contiguity with the III Reich. The narrow Polish access was known as the corridor. Gdansk, as a port city, had a polyglot citizenry among whom there were many German merchants and artisans. During the period of the dismemberment of Poland, Gdansk and Szczecin were entirely under German domination. Despite the fact that Germany lost World War I, it was always a prime objective of German policy to cut Poland's access to the sea by regaining full control over Gdansk and the corridor. Hitler used the alleged mistreatment of the German minority in Gdansk as the excuse to start World War II. He faced Poland with an ultimatum demanding the return of Gdansk to Germany. Poland refused and World War II became the long nightmare of Europe which ultimately engulfed the entire globe. At the end of the World War II, Poland regained both of these ports in a state of near total destruction.

This historical narrative about Gdansk indicates that you will visit not only a beautiful city, carefully restored, but a shrine to Poland's fierce dedication to a free access to its sea, the Baltic.

Whereas before we suggested that you hire a car and driver for your visit to Gdansk and its surroundings, we insist you do. You do have the option of flying to Gdansk and hiring a driver there, but you would miss an interesting trip. In Gdansk there are three excellent hotels: the Hevelius, the Novotel, and the Psejdon, which has a very good restaurant. Be sure to make a reservation before you leave Warsaw.

The city is full of beautiful buildings, monuments, fountains, good restaurants and charming coffee houses. The main street is Dluga (Dlooga) with a mixture of late medieval and early Renaissance architecture. Gdansk's vibrant economy was based on grain exports and the manufacture of unique and highly prized furniture, magnificent silver ornaments and flatware. But the real native treasure of Gdansk and the northern Baltic coast was and is still amber. This semiprecious stone ranges in color from a deep yellowish brown to yellow. It was in demand by high-born ladies of the Roman Empire and retains its attractiveness to this date. There are many stores which sell it and in order to take it out of the country, it has to be paid for in dollars. Amber is not only used for jewelry. There are also many magnificent sculptures (miniatures) made of amber.

While you are in Gdansk, if you can find it, we suggest that you buy a unique alcoholic drink that contains flakes of gold. Its name is Danziger Goldwasser. That name is one of the few concessions Poles will make to the German aspect of Gdansk's history.

As for Gdansk, we suggest that you avail yourself of the services of an experienced guide. There is too much to see and simply listing it does not do justice to its beauty.

But, as you view the magnificent Gothic structure which was the Council House you might want to think of the origins of our American form of democracy. We always like to point to ancient Athens and the golden age of Pericles as being the roots of our democracy. Perhaps, in a philosophical sense, they are. But in fact, our form of government first (republican, and thereafter democratic) originated in the port cities of northern Europe, from Amsterdam to Gdansk. Port cities were always fiercely independent and very conscious of their importance to the land-locked ·kingdoms, which without them could not prosper.

Very aware of that power, the citizens of Gdansk demanded and received privileges denied to most cities of Poland. A citizen of Gdansk was subject to the laws, ordinances, and taxes imposed by the city council. If the council decided to share the tax revenues with the crown, it was free to do so. But it was not compelled. At one point in the history of Poland, Gdansk refused Poland's Royal Navy entry into the port, and the navy sailed away.

Gdansk gained fame as one of Europe's great centers of furniture manufacture, weaving and silver artisanship. All items were very ornate and judging by their dimensions were destined for huge mansions, not of the aristocracy, but of the merchant oligarchy. Certainly there were abuses of power and expressions of great discontent voiced by the poor artisans and day laborers. But that does not diminish the principle and value of having a representative government, a constitution, and a rule of law, especially if you think about the fact that in the areas surrounding Gdansk a king could say "off with their heads" and the heads fell. The visitor gains the impression that the citizens of Gdansk are proud of their past and confident of their future. The citizens of Gdansk have affirmed their deep devotion to Catholicism by building the largest church in Europe, the Church of Our Lady, with brick and mortar. There is a symbolism in this particular choice of building material. It was brick and mortar that laid the foundations of our civilization, in the literal sense of the word. The identical symbolism is present in the monumental steel crosses which commemorate the workers killed in a confrontation with a government which claimed to be the government representing the proletariat. That confrontation occurred in 1970. An identical confrontation took place in 1979, but the results were different. This time the workers, the intellectuals, the peasants from all of Poland joined the workers of Gdansk and Solidarity came into existence. In 1989 Solidarity veterans took over the governance of all of Poland. If there is such a phenomenon as historical destiny, Gdansk was, by its history, destined to be the birthplace of Solidarity and the root of Poland's new democracy.

One real advantage of being in a port city lying on the estuary of a river is the ease with which it is possible to take a trip on a sightseeing boat. Gdansk has very comfortable boats from which you can view the port and the truly imposing silos built in the 14th and 15th century when Poland was the greatest grain exporter in Europe. The massive buildings, the loading docks, the moorings for the sailing ships are so well kept that they seem to be waiting for customers. The Gdansk Shipping Company on 4 Wartka Street (telephone: 31-19-75) can give you information about the boat excursions and sell you the tickets.

One adventure that we recommend wholeheartedly is an excursion by hydrofoil along the coastline, and if you have the time, you can take the ferry to Sweden.

For those who prefer to walk and sightsee, we recommend in addition to Dluga Street, the Royal Road, which starts at the High Gate, for ages the main entrance into the city. The Royal Road adorned with colorful and sumptuous burgher houses comes to an end at the main Town Hall, now housing the Museum of the City of Gdansk. It is really worth visiting and from its tower you can enjoy a panoramic view of the city.

The architectural uniqueness of Gdansk lies in the mixture of styles ranging from the early Gothic to late Renaissance and a magnificent Baroque chapel. According to historical documents Gdansk was already an important port in 997 AD with the name of Gyddayzc on the *Via Mercantorum* (the merchants' route).

In the middle ages there used to be a saying that "City air makes free." This was true. According to medieval custom, sometimes even written as a law, an indentured peasant was allowed to become a free citizen of a town if he managed to elude capture for a year and a day. Judging by the contemporary revolutions of eastern Europe, which all began in Gdansk, the old saying should be modified to "Gdansk air makes free."

The visual opulence of Gdansk is a good reason to talk about shopping in Poland. While the country is in the process of restructuring its economy to be more effective and market oriented, the government has had to freeze wages and allow prices to fluctuate according to the laws of supply and demand. In a country where labor is cheap—and Poland's workers receive very low wages—objects which require a lot of work, or to use the economic term, objects which are labor intensive, tend to be inexpensive.

You can not help but notice magnificent furniture in the palaces you visited and in Gdansk itself. If you have a yen for exquisite replicas of any style or period furniture from the Renaissance to Danish Modern, you can have it made in Poland. The price will be very advantageous even if you include the cost of shipping. It would not be worth your while to buy furniture, or anything else that is mass marketed in the United States. Such items will cost you more in Poland than if you were to buy the identical item in your favorite shopping mall and found out that it was "Manufactured in Poland." Our recommendation for shopping in Poland is limited to high ticket items such as silver table settings, products made of crystal and antiques. Occasionally you might find clothing you like, sweaters, blouses, tailor-made suits for men and women, hand-made leather accessories and jewelry. We are not in a position to recommend specific stores where you can find these items, but if you are staying in a first class hotel, you can ask either the manager of the Pewex (the dollar store), which will have a store in your hotel, or the concierge. But your driver is the best source of information.

The best furniture factory for period furniture is in Henrykowo, very near Warsaw. Antiques are sold through Dessa stores which can be found in most major Polish cities. But, as free enterprise takes root on Poland's soil, you will find boutiques and luxury stores as you walk down the main avenues of big cities like Warsaw, Krakow, Gdansk and others we are yet to describe. We are ourselves looking forward to a shopping expedition to Poland.

Gdansk is actually at the center of three cities, Gdynia and Sopot being the other two. During the inter-war period (1918–1939), Poland poured millions of dollars into creating Gdynia, a subsidiary port to accommodate the needs of Poland, and built fortifications to protect Gdansk. One of these fortresses was Westerplatte, which withstood the direct bombardment of Hitler's most powerful battleships for 21 days. Long after all of Poland was defeated, that fort continued to defend itself. When it fell there were almost no survivors. Heroism must be known and never forgotten, but in itself it is not a tourist attraction. Thus there is not much to see in Gdynia, but Sopot is worth a visit.

It used to be a very elegant spa with a magnificient Grand Hotel, beautiful beaches and a casino. What is really left are the beautiful beaches. They are delightful and you could rent a boat to appreciate them and the sea. Unfortunately, the water is so polluted that swimming is not allowed. While there is nothing really to compensate for the pleasures of a dip in the ocean, the walks along the beaches and the parks are an acceptable substitute.

The region around Gdansk abounds with worthwhile sights. One of them is Malbork, the best preserved Gothic fortress of the Teutonic Knights. As a visitor, sitting quietly under the towers of the Marlbork castle, or on the shores of the Baltic, it is difficult to sense that you are seeing the rising curtain of changes. The citizens of Gdansk are probably aware of what is likely to happen. There are already plans to extend the fabulous German autobahn across from Germany to "East Prussia' and Kaliningrad which will become the largest port on the Baltic and a fearsome rival for Gdansk. Just as a historical footnote—in the late 1930's Germany proposed to build an authobahn through Poland to their Konigsberg. The refusal of sovereign Poland to allow that route to be built was the quiet first shot of World War II. It was the shot that was not heard. Now Poland has agreed to the building of that route because Poland—to survive—must become a member of the European community. A community which will be under German hegemony—not by force of arms but by force of the German mark.

The year 1992 will undoubtedly be remembered in history as the year of the greatest social and political hurricane that swept Eastern and Central Europe since the dawn of modern history. The entire region is digging out from under ruins of that which was detested and that which was loved. Destruction is never selective. Gdansk and the entire region around it lived through horrendous cataclysms of invasions, fires, occupation, and ferocious wars. It now has to find a new place for itself, a new reason for existence, a new vision for its future.

CHAPTER THIRTEEN

The Pleasures of the Unexpected

As you leave the high culture and romantic history of Gdansk and begin to travel in an easterly direction, through Prussia, past the bunker where Hitler should have died in the July 20, 1944, assassination attempt, you enter the Mazurian Lake region which borders on the Soviet Union, a region of Europe that requires a specific mindset to be fully appreciated.

In every highly touted tourist area of the world, you get to see what you expect. In Rome it's the ancient Forum Romanum and the Basilica of St. Peter; in Athens it is the Acropolis; in France it's the Eiffel Tower. Those are magnificent sights to behold, but their splendor confirms what you expect.

Years of residence in the great and small cities in the West have dulled our senses. Most of us are unaccustomed to a type of natural beauty that hits us over the head like a sledge

115

hammer and proclaims to our senses that what we are seeing in fact is beautiful. And as often happens, the beauty masks an underlying brutality.

When you view the magnificent pyramids of Egypt, you probably do not think of the thousands who died building them. Yet, the pyramids are beautiful, majestic, and give us a feeling of pride in belonging to a species capable of creating grandeur.

As you enter a museum devoted to abstract art, the wildest expressions of an artist's imagination stun you, possibly disorient you, but as you surrender your senses to the power of the art you begin to sense its beauty—it "does something" to you. It forces you to see in a way you are not accustomed to seeing.

Traveling through the eastern region of Poland presents a unique challenge of seeing simultaneously the grandeur of historical structures and the beauty of abstractions. They are not man-made abstractions, but abstractions of nature, untouched by human hands or the artist's imagination. You will move from the pre-history of Europe to the present in the span of a few days.

The great wave of human migration from the Siberian plains to the walls of Rome, which occurred during the first centuries of our millennium, destroyed the high civilization of Rome and plunged all of Latinized Europe into a period we call the dark ages, from which we are probably just beginning to emerge. A huge movement of peoples leaves residues which defy explanation. To this date, for example, we cannot explain how the Basques managed to wedge themselves in between highly civilized northern Spain and southern France. How did they maintain their language, their fierce sense of independence, and their complex culture?

There is a similar phenomenon in eastern Poland. It is not as spectacular as the case of the Basques, but it is equally mysterious. In the sea of tribes among whom the Teutons and the Huns and the Goths were the most aggressive, there were smaller tribes with impossible names like the Kaszubians (pronounced "Cashoobians") and the Jatzvigians (pronounced "Yatzvigians"). There are remnants of them left in small isolated hamlets of eastern Poland. They live in mud hovels, are crude and brutal, and speak a language which is virtually incomprehensible even to the Polish linguist. The strongest among such tribes were the Prussians.

In the 13th century, when Poland was beginning to become a unified Christian kingdom, one of the powerful dukes felt threatened by the pagan Prussians and invited the Teutonic Knights to help him. The plausible excuse for this request was to help overcome the resistance of the Prussians to convert to Catholicism. It was the sacred duty of the Knights to help spread Christianity and to protect missionaries, churches and monasteries. The Knights eagerly undertook the task.

The Teutonic Knights were a sight to behold. Mounted, wearing silvery armor, they also draped themselves with white capes embroidered with huge black crosses. With their superior armor and knowledge of strategy, they defeated all armies, pillaged the countryside and laid waste to entire areas. The only other place in Europe that suffered equal "knightly" devastation was southern France, where during the Albigencien Crusades of the 14th century, the flourishing culture of Provence was so thoroughly devastated that to this date the soil is barren, the countryside empty.

To secure their hold on the occupied territory, the Teutonic Knights built imposing defensive castles of which the Castle of Marlbork, still intact, is worth an extended visit. Most of the churches built by the Knights of the Cross (as they were known), were Gothic in style. The Knights attempted to capture in the mid-15th century the Frombork Castle, whose defenses were designed and planned by Copernicus, who lived and died there. The castle withstood the siege.

The Knights of the Cross subdued the Prussians and succeeded in Germanizing them. They did not bother with the other smaller tribes who, thus, retained their identity.

The Polish kings, perceiving the insatiable ambitions of the Knights, waged constant warfare against them. The Polish armed forces succeeded in stopping the expansionist drive of the Teutonic Knights by defeating them soundly at the battle of Grunwald in 1410. The spectacular monument you see on the battlefield is one of the most revered among all of Poland's historical monuments. Despite this defeat, the Knights of the Cross continued to wage war against Poland until 1525, when the order was secularized and its Grand Master Hohenzollern, ancestor of the German Imperial family, had to pay homage to the king of Poland and acknowledge Poland's lordship over all of Prussia.

The Hohenzollerns prospered, became kings of Prussia, and in 1870 the emperors of Germany. They renounced their subservience to the Polish crown in the 17th century and in the late 18th century participated in the partitions of Poland in which they not only gained Prussia and Gdansk, but also the western provinces of Poland, including, for a short time, Warsaw. The Hohenzollerns owe their good fortune to the fact that Poland's foreign policy was directed by papal influence to defend Christendom from the growing power of Muscovy and the constant threat posed by the bellicose Ottoman Empire.

Poland was not strong enough to fight battles on two fronts: on the east against the growing power of the Russian kingdom and on the southeast against the constant warfare with the armies of the sultan, the actual title of the ruler of the Ottoman Empire. Thus while the kings of Poland focused on the east, the Germanic powers were free to undermine Poland's influence in the west. In the 18th century, two centuries prior to the Hitler-Stalin pact, the Hohenzollerns of Prussia and the Romanoffs of Russia (at that point ruled by Catherine the Great, a German princess) made peace and subjugated one part of the Polish population to a relentless policy of Germanization, and the other part to a brutally implemented policy of Russification.

The Poles resisted both attempts successfully, but the German attempt was the more subtle and dangerous of the two. During World War II, Hitler changed the policy of Germanization into a policy of eradication of all that was Polish. Stalin changed the policy of Russification to murder and resettlement in distant Siberia. The Romanoffs failed, the Hitlerites failed, but the Poles paid a tremendous price for their right to be Poles and to be free.

Today Gdansk is Polish and so is a part of Prussia. During

the general territorial settlement that followed the Allied victory in World War II, Poland regained some western German lands it owned during the first six centuries of its existence, and gave up to the Soviet Union provinces it had conquered in wars against Muscovy, the Tartar hordes and the Ottoman Empire. The adjustment of Poland's frontiers is still a painful subject for many Poles, whose cultural and economic influence brought many of the lost eastern lands out of an existence of ignorance and poverty to a level that made their present existence possible.

But we started this chapter to talk about beauty and not gore. Unfortunately these are frequently linked. The indominable human spirit needs freedom to create beauty and to appreciate the beauty nature placed at its disposal.

The beauty we are inviting you to share is the legacy of the retreating Scandinavian glacier which eons ago left in its wake 3,000 lakes, rivulets and a soil fertile enough for a rich and varigated flora and fauna.

Wherever there is an abundance of lakes, there is a richness of vegetation. The land is relatively flat; excellent for jogging, long walks, cross-country skiing, hunting and long riding excursions. The area is well equipped with children's playgrounds, adequate emergency medical facilities, and comfortable hotels, inns and guest rooms. However, in comparison to Miami, you will be roughing it here.

Lakes are a permanent invitation to sailing, fishing, swimming, and just lazing on grassy banks. Poland manufactures excellent camping equipment, which can be acquired, and is so compact that it is easy to transport to the many camping sites found throughout Poland. But the pride of the Polish sporting equipment industry is its boats, ranging from kayaks to sailboats. In winter this area of Poland offers superb conditions for iceboating; a world class competition was held there. Fishing used to be excellent, but due to pollution problems, fish are less abundant. Poland produces very good fishing rods, but we are told that the reels are faulty and occasionally there are problems in acquiring the proper hooks and bait. If fishing is important to you, we recommend that you bring with you the equipment you are used to.

Since this area is the most attractive summer playground for young Polish families, the accommodations are likely to be over-crowded during the summer months. We suggest, therefore, that you contact Orbis well in advance of your departure and indicate that you wish to visit the Mazurian Lake area. Orbis maintains a number of one-family chalets which are fully equipped, spacious, comfortable, and provided with maid service for all household chores. These accommodations are favored by the Swedes and the Germans, the most numerous group of foreign tourists in the area. Since they are return guests each year they might have a priority on these accommodations. There are, however, a number of Orbis hotels in the area and quite a few Orbis-supervised private facilities that would also meet your needs.

If you happen to be a member of a profession, i.e., teaching, writing, musical, theatrical, medical, scientific, etc., you might qualify for room in the spacious accommodations maintained by professional organizations for members. There are provisions for "guest members." Again you would have to find out from Orbis where the main offices of such organizations are located and write a letter to the president giving him the precise dates when you would like to stay in their facility, how many will be in your party and what your qualifications are to entitle you to stay there. In the same letter, offer to pay the equivalent you would have to pay for an Orbis-run facility. Chances are very good that you will be invited and treated like an honored guest. Frequently these summer rest places are used for seminars. If the topic of one which is scheduled falls within your area of expertise, you may offer to give a paper. Incidentally, this is one of the best ways of meeting the very pinnacle of Poland's intellectuals. And while we mention this in connection with the Mazurian Lakes region, you might want to take advantage of such opportunities in other areas of Poland, notably in the Tatra region.

During your stay in the Mazurian Lake area you should visit the museum of folk buildings, located in Olsztynek (pronounced "Olshtynek") on the E 81 highway. The museum contains the richest and most varied examples of east European wooden architecture. There is no similar collection to be found elswhere in Europe. You will also see the dwellings that served for homes for the poorest of Polish peasants. Families lived in an enclosed area, shaped like a cone. Through the peak escaped the smoke from the open fire used for cooking and warmth. The walls were usually a combination of hides, woven twigs, and straw. When the fire was not lit, the only light for the space came from an opening in the wall, over which a fish bladder stretched. The family, along with the one pig or goat, shared the same space. Their life style, their brutality and avariciousness have been masterfully described in Jerzy Kosinski's book *The Painted Bird*.

The jewel of the entire area is the Augustynow Forest. It was one of the largest in Poland and was cut in half by the Soviet frontier following World War II. The pine forest is the last remnant of the huge forests that covered all of northeastern Europe. There are many lakes in that forest and they are interconnected by canals. You can take an 80-mile photographer's safari through this area if you are interested.

And now the time has come to return to Warsaw. Along the road, look for stork nests atop wooden roofs of peasant homes. The storks build their nests close to the chimneys and return to the same nest every year. Folklore has it that when a stork returns, a baby will be born to the household. This is probably the origin of the tale of the stork delivering babies. There are many babies in Poland's countryside.

CHAPTER FOURTEEN

The Cradle of Art

We Americans live in a most peculiar century. Many of us are glued to "the tube," awed by fantastic simulations produced by the high technology of our times, yet we spend millions of dollars for a vase or a clock produced by an old master. It does not dawn on us that new masters are still around and in time will become as revered as the old masters, whose value we express not through admiration of the intrinsic aesthetic of their work, but through payment of mountains of gold for it.

Old masters need three things: talent, time and patrons. In certain instances they also need more efficient tools.

Poland, a culture that contributed to the beauty of the world for a millennium, abounds with old masters that are still alive and still capable of producing exquisite masterpieces. The reason they still exist is in itself paradoxical. They can be found in Poland, and generally in the less industrialized areas of the world, precisely because they are less industrialized. In translation this means that people have to think what it is that they really want to produce, and people with talent think how to produce a useful object and imbue it with beauty. A useful object is any object that enriches our lives, emotions, senses, and dreams.

In order to take advantage of Polish artisans, craftsmen, and artists, a certain amount of preparation is required. As Americans we have a specific sense of design and our own notion of beauty, unless, of course, we are enamored with a period of history and would like to have facsimile reproductions of objects produced in that period, i.e., Louis XIV, Empire or George III. We have mentioned that you can have this type of furniture produced for you by the artisans working in the furniture factory in Henrykowo which is very close to Warsaw. But buying an object that looks like an antique— no matter how exquisite the copy is—implies a certain bashfulness, as if we were afraid to express our own tastes, as if we were hesitant to buy the unusual. Art is a bridge to the past, but it is also the arrow pointing to the future. Especially now that the political shackles have been removed, the Polish artist can release the pent up and suppressed creativity. This explosion of freedom will ignite an expansion in all the activities that come under the heading of art.

It is a pathetic commentary on our sense of the artistic that we assign a lower classification to folk art as opposed to real art. There would be no real art if there were no folk art. Poland has a style which incorporates the three basic elements of Poland: its history, its faith and its all pervasive love of nature. If you like art, and you want a lasting memento of your visit to Poland, select and buy the art that somehow will mean "Poland" to you. Art is by definition unrestricted in the way it chooses to express itself; it frequently is found in objects that help perform a useful function. Utilitarian art is still art. Poland's peasants developed magnificent utilitarian art. It is hard to believe that the common soup ladle made out of wood, its handle adorned by intricate chiseled designs, is a work of art. And what is hard to believe is the lacework of wood around the hole at the top of the handle that makes it possible to hang it on the kitchen wall. Our soup ladle is twenty years old. It aged gracefully, the wood acquired a sheen, a patina as evidence of its years and recognition of its services. We bought it at a peasant market and we paid the asking price: two dollars.

One of the most surprising pieces of art we have purchased was a table made from a tree stump, and the roots of the same tree. Although it was created very recently, we in fact bought an antique. A friend of ours could decipher the age of the tree by counting the rings on our table top. The tree was 150 years old. These rings formed a design of unconscious beauty. Each ring is clearly visible, separated and of different hue and seemingly different texture. The table top is protected by we don't know how many coats of clear shellac, is heat resistant and displays no rings. It does not obscure the design. The legs of the table are made from the peeled roots of the tree. They are so powerful and so solid that you know they could anchor and sustain a massive tree. The table radiates warmth because the artist balanced the size of the top with the height and massiveness of the roots. You can find such tables and other furnishings in little stores surrounding the Old Town Market in Warsaw, at the Sukiennice of Krakow, and at some of the peasant markets. Our apartment is too small to buy other pieces like chests of drawers, huge storage boxes, and beautifully carved but really comfortable wooden chairs. We paid $50 for the table—an indication of the prices—they may be a bit higher today.

You might be lucky and the owner of the store may actually be the artist. If he is not, try to find out where the artist lives and if he happens to be in a village that you are passing through, or near the road you are traveling, stop in to see him. Do not go because he will sell you a piece for less, but a wood sculptor's studio is fascinating and you could find something that is even more striking and more to your liking. If the owner of the store is the artist, he/she might invite you to visit his studio and you might discover an object you really want or even commission a piece from the artist. No matter how often you visit an artist's studio, it usually turns out to be a memorable experience.

The other art objects are wooden sculptures. We found a wooden sculpture, about 20 inches high, which looks just like a clean wooden log, but when it is properly lit, you can clearly see the figure of an old Jew in traditional garb. The title of the sculpture is "The Vanishing Jew." It stands in our window and you can see the statue when the sun is at its back. A truly remarkable piece of work.

Poland has an abundance of silver, high quality woods, crystal, semi-precious stones, and unusual fabrics. This array of raw material gives your imagination room to play. And time to play. Craftsman are slow and deliberate in their work. If you want a silver service for twelve or twenty-four, including globlets, soup tureens and all that goes with it, you have to allow time for it to be finished to his satisfaction. It will take less time to have a modern design set than it will to have a faithfully executed highly baroque design. When you are in Poland, you can take the artisan with you to one of the royal palaces, museums, or a library which has old illuminated books and show him what you want. What you show him, you will get. Your greatest problem will be to find the trustworthy artisan. We suggest that you ask the custodian of a palace, or the librarian, or the curator of the museum. Poland, because it was so devastated by the war, has art restorers of world renown and you can be certain to find the proper one.

When Florence was devastated by a flood and the famous Medici Mausoleum was severely damaged, Poland furnished the crew to do the restoration. Restorers are by definition artisans. They are not difficult to find and they work first for love and secondly for money. You will have to pay for the cost of the silver in dollars; you should pay the artisan also in dollars, or perhaps invite him/her to come to the U.S., where they can make a fortune. If a unique, hand carved place setting would cost $4,000 in New York, it would cost perhaps $500 to $600 in Poland. These prices are quoted as examples only so you can find or commission striking place settings at the lower end of the price range.

One of Poland's greatest exports is hand-painted porcelain plates. On his recent visit to Poland, the king of Spain ordered a full service for 24 people. One of the best porcelain manufacturers is in Wloclawek, a couple of hours away from Warsaw. You could stop there on your way to Gdansk. But we recommend that you do not mix sightseeing with a real shopping expedition. Determine before you go to Poland what you may like to buy and then take the time to find the best source and visit it. This planning will not interfere with your impulse buying.

You have a choice in goblets. They can be in clear or colored crystal, and they can be silver encrusted with semi-precious stones.

A place setting needs three other components that bring out its full beauty: a damask tablecloth, suitably embroidered with handmade lace, the right table and chairs, and the candelabras. A period setting suffers from electric light directly overhead, even if the light is a crystal chandelier. (Incidentally, they make magnificent chandeliers in Poland because Poland has bronze, brass and crystal.) Candelabras come in so many shapes, forms and styles that they defy enumeration. You would do well to bring a picture, or leave it up to the artisan to make them in keeping with the style of the place settings, or take what he has. As the matter of fact, if you want to furnish your house or condo, it is worth your time to go to Poland with this specific purpose in mind. First visit the country and become familiar with it, find out what it has to offer in the way of things you would like to get and then go back and shop. Even if you include the cost of a round trip fare and a ten-day stay in Poland with the cost of transporting your acquisitions, you will still save at least 40 percent of the cost of similar objects in the U.S.

We know that American shoppers are impatient. They want to pay and have delivery immediately. That will not work in Poland. You might even have to send the artisan some tools, especially grinding wheels, that are currently not available in Poland. But measure your pleasure in terms of the many years of enjoyment you will get and in the fact that these will become real heirlooms for your family.

The other truly great shopping expedition is for furniture. It is difficult to describe the warmth, the sheen, the elegance of an Empire style desk, inlaid with a mosaic of different woods, each carefully placed to produce the effect of a rose in bloom, or perfect geometric pattern. The corners will be handcrafted bronze or brass ornaments. The handles on the drawers will be completely unobtrusive and fit into a groove to be out of the way of the writer sitting at the desk. The legs will have a graceful curve ending probably in the form of a brass paw. The wood is durable and except for wanton destruction, will wear well for centuries. Yes, there will be hidden compartments, and each drawer can be locked. Be sure to have duplicate keys made, because once this desk is in your house, you will be hard pressed to find an expert to replace a lost key.

There are three pieces of furniture that make a study. We will however omit having a library built in Poland. It would be too cumbersome to ship and even if your condo is huge, we assure it will not fit, unless you have 24 foot ceilings, the appropriate circular stairs to reach the top shelves and the ornate crystal panes fitting the doors that enclose the shelves.

The three pieces we have in mind are either petit point, gilded arm chairs, or more masculine leather highback chairs, separated by an appropriate table for sipping brandy, and a rug. Rug weaving is still an art in Poland and a real Persian rug can be purchased in Poland in antique shops which we will describe below.

The furniture factory is in Henrykowo (Enrikovo), in the vicinity of Warsaw. The factory manufactures facsimiles of any period furniture you may desire. But it is a factory and not the work of individual artisans. We recommend it, however, because they have all the material required to do a first rate job. Now a facsimile is not a copy. A facsimile is an exact, precise creation of a piece of furniture as it was manufactured at the time when it first appeared. Some modern short cuts will be taken, but not in a noticeable way. It will take a real expert to determine when it was made. The give away will probably be the method of fastening the wood together. A desk as we described above would cost a minimum of $30,000 to $40,000 in New York. It would be the envy of the highest priced attorney in the big city. Delivered to New York, this desk would cost approximately $10,000, when purchased in Poland.

The packing, shipping formalities and delivery to your home will be handled very expeditiously by Hartwig, a private firm, over a century old, very experienced and completely reliable. Hartwig has an office in every major town. The main office is in Warsaw.

It is quite possible that some of you readers work for large law firms and global corporations. They spend millions furnishing executive offices, conference rooms and lavish reception areas. They could find what they are looking for in Poland. Poland abounds in original art. None of it is really expensive and a lot is produced by primitive peasant wood carvers. We are not experts in oil paintings, but we have been told that some of the modern abstractionists are world-scale. If you have a chance to visit Soho in New York City, you can see the work of many Polish painters who came to the U.S. during the last decade. However, Poland has superb graphic artists who continuously exhibit in the myriads of galleries found in all of the major cities we have mentioned.

If, as we are, you are insecure about art, go to the Academy of Fine Art in Warsaw or Krakow and find a young student, preferably in torn jeans, long haired, wearing a stained tee shirt and ask him to show you the best of the graphic artists. If that makes you uncomfortable, ask the custodian of the Museum of Posters in Wilanow, and she will recommend an appropriate guide. To select art you do not have to speak Polish. Just follow the guide and look at what he is pointing at and let your taste be your buying conscience.

CHAPTER FIFTEEN

A Cradle for Artists

The freedom Poland now enjoys, the exuberance of a people allowed to chart their own course, created an atmosphere, a cultural ambiance, which should act like a magnet for artists from all countries, and especially from the metropolitan areas of the United States. The high rents, the physical dangers lurking in the sections where affordable housing might be available, and the tremendous difficulty in finding space to exhibit their art ought to make Poland attractive to serious, dedicated and above all talented young people. If they have these characteristics, they will be welcome into the most attractive group of people in Poland.

The photographers, painters, graphic artists and musicians and even writers might explore Poland first as tourists and then as long-term residents. By "long-term" we mean six months to two years. If they go as tourists, they should contact the Polish Society of Touring, located on Narbuta (Narboota) Street 27A, in Warsaw and the Polish Tourism Agency (acronym PTTK, and known internationally as It). Their main office is located at the Plac Zamkowy 1/13 Warsaw, 27 telephone 27 00 00. Actually to call Warsaw, you have to dial 011, 48, 22, and then the actual telephone number. Call or contact the appropriate Polish agency listed in this book in the section entitled "Almanac for Travelers," only after you have made the necessary financial arrangements to stay in Poland for six months or more and have really decided to go.

If you can save $3,000, you will have enough for your air fare and for a year in Poland. Assuming it will cost you $600 for your ticket, you will have $2,400 left over. The rent for your room can not be higher than $80 per month. Of course, you would be living with a family. Many Polish families are used to having guests in their houses for long periods. Your privacy will be respected. All you need to do is to find out the rhythm of life that particular family practices and arrange your use of the bathroom and kitchen accordingly. After a period of feeling strange, you will become a member of the family. Share some of the things you will be able to buy like instant coffee, soap, and detergents, and occasionally bring some flowers, cosmetics and the little paraphernalia of life that makes living easier and more pleasant. As a dividend you will learn some Polish and you will get a lot of advice on where to go and what to see. But no one will intrude on your life.

We did it for one year and it worked out really well. To have as much fun as we had, we urge you to go to Orbis, or to the Polish cultural attache a few months before you want to leave. Ask him for the name of the director of the artistic association with which you would want to be affiliated. Every classification of the huge field identified as art has an association, i.e., photographers, sculptors, painters, writers, actors, dancers, etc. The cultural attache will be able to give you the current address and may have some suggestions of his own.

You may be puzzled by our suggestion that a writer go to a

country whose language, customs, history and social conventions are unknown to him. The answer is simple: He/She will have a private room and complete peace of mind for one solid year. A luxury very, very few writers can enjoy in this country. Most are forced to take all sorts of odd or temporary jobs to make ends meet. Imagine being able to knock yourself out for one year to save $3,000 and then being able to enjoy one year during which you will only have to do that which you want to do. Your social life will have a dimension of pleasure hard to find in this country.

You will find all the supplies you need in today's Poland. Take with you only those implements which you consider indispensable to the exercise of your craft, especially if you are a sculptor. If you are used to working with a word processor, you can acquire one cheaper in Poland than here. However, since you have already made the investment, you will probably want to ship it ahead of you to the association under whose auspices you will be working. Incidentally, if you are a visual artist and good, the association will try very hard to help you exhibit in one of the many galleries operating in Poland's larger cities. Also, do not disdain the U.S. cultural attache in Warsaw. The individual assigned to this post is usually invited to all *vernisages,* all new theatrical and musical events, and is well known in Poland's artistic circles and would be willing to introduce you and help you arrange an exhibit if only in the lobby of the U.S. Embassy.

We purposely left the best for the last. If you happen to be a film maker or are interested in any aspect of film making, we urge you to write to the Film Center and School in Lodz. The Polish cultural attache will give you the specifics. That center happens to have a wonderful international reputation, not only because Wajda and Polanski got their start there and Hanna-Barbera makes most of its animation cartoons there, but because of the very high standards of training the center requires from its participants. You will have to bring with you the video tape you prefer and your own equipment. We do not suggest that you lug a motion picture camera with you; that you can get at the center. The film industry is booming and you might even get to work on a production. The director knows enough English to yell at you if you goof and to say something that could pass for a compliment if you are good.

We can not overemphasize the need to plan. Without a detailed plan, you will be frustrated and waste half of your time making the arrangements you should have thought of before you left. Unless you can get an American grant, it will take you at least one year of frugal, very frugal living to save $3,000, and you can use that time to make all the arrangements by mail. You can also use that time to learn the Polish language. The State University of New York at New Paltz offers immersion courses in Polish. They are on weekends and are not expensive. You can also buy tapes that will teach you the language. Or, if you are in New York, you can go to the Polish section, find the local priest and offer to swap English lessons for Polish lessons. We are fairly certain that you will find a way to learn enough Polish for your needs and you will become fluent after you have acquired a basic knowledge. You can follow this suggestion in any city which has a large Polish population.

In addition, the Polish government offers six-weeks courses in Polish at the Jagellonian University of Krakow. This provision used to be restricted to people of Polish origin. We think that this restriction has been waived. The tuition and lodging used to be nominal. Perhaps they still are.

Your basic wardrobe for going to Poland is the one you are wearing. Take extra socks and underwear; everything else you can buy in Poland. Women should take their cosmetics and ample supply of hygiene products, and everyone should take various antihistamines and cold remedies, if you use them. A hot water bottle may also come in handy. Bring a good radio. All other musical apparatus can be purchased in Warsaw.

Drugs are on the market. The penalties for either use or possession are draconic. The enforcement of anti-drug laws falls within the province of military jurisdiction. A trial by a military court-martial is swift, the penalties severe, and there is no appeal process. The U.S. Embassy will see to it that you have legal counsel if you need it, but will not interfere on your behalf. The only thing you can hope for is that the Poles, after conviction, will expel you from their country. This is a gesture of good will on their part. They are not obliged to do it.

We are finished with all of this "paternal" advice and now we will visit two more cities which are important in this all too rapid overview of Poland.

CHAPTER SIXTEEN

Tale of Two Cities: Poznan and Wroclaw

History has been and is center stage in every large Polish city. In most of Europe's great cities, history is a cherished monument expressed by the love and care lavished on its monuments. In the two cities we recommend for overnight visits, history is a living monument; it pulsates through the squares, the ever present beautiful churches, palaces, and the residences of magnates and patricians. But the best, most apt metaphor for Poland is to be found a very short distance from Poznan near the small town of Rogalin. Its main attraction is a park which consists of about 900 oaks, which are supposed to be over a thousand years old or more. The largest one measures 27 feet around the trunk. Close to the giant oak are two others, somewhat smaller in diameter and height. They are supposed to represent the three great Slavic tribes: Lech, Czech, and Rus, the legendary brothers who created Poland, Bohemia, and Russia. Although Poland is named after the Polanyi tribe, its actual ancestors belonged to the Lech tribe. The sultans of the Ottoman Empire referred to Poland as Lechistan. And even when Poland was partitioned and had no independence, the sultan of the Great Empire of the East on state occasions, when all ambassadors present in Istanbul had to come to court, never failed to ask for the ambassador from Lechistan. When told that he was absent, the sultan would smile and say "Soon he will come." The "soon" took a century and a half but there is now an ambassador from Lechistan in Istanbul. Poland is a mighty oak. Poland lives even through times when it is justifiable to wonder if it is worth living. Poland, like the mighty oak, is growing, proud and optimistic. It sprouts new branches and every year covers itself with new leaves just like the oak. Walesa's first name is Lech. There is a chance that his integrity, his respect for humanity and his search for a peace formula will grow like the mighty tree. Incidentally "Lech" is a very popular name for boys.

Poznan lies astride the Warta (Varta) River and was always an important trading center. Like most of Poland's great cities, it is about a thousand years old and in that period of time was devastated innumerable times and always rebuilt. It is truly amazing that a country of economic hardships, of food and housing shortages, always had the money, time, and effort required to reconstruct. We are in awe of the builders of Poznan and of Wroclaw. Many of the people who worked on restoration had to learn anew crafts long forgotten. And no one begrudged the expense of restoring a palace which most of the time is used as a museum. Americans especially will be astounded by this love of history, by this desire to keep the continuity of history alive for present and future generations.

When it comes to preserving history, Poland is a wealthy country. The instant you get to Poznan, you will have the feeling that there is something Germanic about it. As a matter of fact, the arterial highway from Warsaw to Poznan was built by the most recent occupiers of Poznan. The Nazi regime incorporated Poznan into the Third Reich. And prior to 1918, Poznan was an integral part of the German Empire. The positive aspects of that long incorporation into Germany are an extensive and solid industrial base, good overland roads, and a rather rare social discipline. The single greatest industrial complex in that region is the Cegelski Factory which produces heavy machinery, rolling stock and modern machine tools. It has a close affiliation with General Electric and Siemens. There are four excellent hotels in Poznan: the Novotel, the Polonez, the Merkury and the Poznan. Be sure to have a reservation in any one of them before you leave Warsaw. The hotel restaurants are good and the service is efficient.

The German overlords of Poznan actually tried to Germanize the city, the entire region under their occupation, but it did not work. There are still visual reminders of the German presence. It is evident, for example, in the neo-classical massive opera house. There was a real effort to Germanize Poznan. Back in 1848 there was an uprising in Poznan and its specific demand was the right to speak Polish and to learn Polish in schools. The people received that right. But under Bismarck, the Iron Chancellor, the process of Germanization continued and so did the resistance to it. There was too much Polish history in Poznan to erase the national consciousness from the minds of the Poles. But Bismarck was really shrewd. He promulgated a law allowing a Polish man to marry a German woman, but *verboten* was a union of a German man with a Polish woman because a Polish mother will bring up a Polish child, no matter what the nationality of the father.

There is a lot to see in and around Poznan. There is a unique Museum of Musical Instruments which contains 750 instruments from all over the world. While we really don't like military museums, we do recommend that you see the

Military Museum which contains beautiful ceremonial armor and a collection of banners from the various uprisings and insurgencies of the 19th century. On the "must see" list is the Poznan Town Hall which was given its current form by Giovanni Quadro of Lugano in 1550. The Town Hall is now the historical museum of Poznan. Try to be on the town square at noon, because precisely at noon you will see and hear a sight that we don't believe can be seen anywhere else in Europe. Precisely at noon two metallic goats will appear above the clock, bang their heads together and disappear back into the building. Serious art students and tourists who really like to see paintings should visit the National Museum. It has very fine collections of art, ranging from the medieval to Modern. Poznan has an excellent university and quite a few centers of scientific research.

But what Poznan is really famous for are its two international fairs, one held in June and devoted primarily to industrial exhibits and one held in September featuring consumer goods. If you are interested in either, you should make your reservation at least six months before you intend to go to Poland. The fairs are very popular.

We have already told you a lot about shopping. Reserve some of it for Poznan, especially if you have a liking for folk art and porcelain.

On the way back to Warsaw—if you are going by car—it is worth your while to stop in Kornik and visit the castle. It contains appealing furniture and good paintings and has an excellent library.

We entitled this chapter "The Tale of Two Cities." Poznan is a Polish city and always was one. Now we shall visit Wroclaw which for many centuries was a German city known as Breslau, but is now a Polish city. It will be featured in headlines yet to be written in connection with the eastern frontiers of a unified Germany.

Wroclaw is one of the great cities of an area identified as Silesia. The Silesians were for centuries an independent dutchy, loosely allied with the Polish kingdom. But as that kingdom began to decline in the 17th and 18th century, Silesia fell more and more under the influence of Prussia. While the eastern part of Silesia was predominantly Polish, the north-western part was closer to Germany politically and culturally. The German name of Wroclaw is Breslau. It was once a thriving city of 650,000 inhabitants, very supportive of Hitler. At the beginning of 1945, when it was already obvious that Germany would lose the war, Hitler declared Breslau to be a fortress. When the Red armies conquered the Festung Breslau, it was utterly destroyed with about 40,000 people left in the ruins.

Breslau/Wroclaw became a Polish city on the basis of a decision by the Allied powers. Stalin insisted on incorporating Polish lands within the Soviet Union and compensating Poland by giving them lands which were part of the German Reich, but to which Poland had an historical claim. Wroclaw was part of that deal. The Polish population in the area opted to leave their homes and move to the western lands or the Recovered Lands, as the area including Wroclaw is currently identified.

The majority of the inhabitants of Wroclaw came from the Polish town of Lwow, which now has the name of Lviv and is capital of the western Ukraine. The people of Lwow share a very high cosmopolitan, European culture. Lwow happened to have been a great center of trade and, so we believe, the only town in Europe inhabited by three of the major branches of Christianity which recognized the pope of Rome as supreme: the Uniates, the Armenian Christians and the Roman Catholics. In addition, Lwow had a significant Jewish population, a highly respected university, a very diversified political life and a most lively, complex, and challenging culture. The Nazis and the Stalinists who occupied Lwow killed the bloom of that sturdy flower, but not its roots. It was transplanted to Wroclaw. Fortunately the transplanted Lwowians were allowed to take part of the fabulous Ossolineum Archives with them and so have the elements of historical continuity. The vast majority of the archives and art treasures were transported to Kiev. They are certainly well preserved and perhaps now may even become accessible.

The ruins of Breslau were inherited by the Poles and transformed into Wroclaw, while remaining faithful to the Renais-

sance style and Germanic architecture in the process of reconstruction. By rebuilding the historical part of Wroclaw as it
was, one of the finest examples of respect Poles have for
culture and monuments of the past was created. Granted that
until the end of the 16th century Wroclaw was part of the
Polish kingdom and one of the most important cities on the
Odra River, no effort was made to change the very visible
Germanic influences.

Of interest to the tourist are the Town Hall and the university. The Town Hall has two splendid rooms: the Prince's
Room and the Aldermen's Room. Both are superb examples of
16th century interior decoration. There are several other interesting Baroque-style buildings attached to the Town Hall.
One of them houses the experimental theater named after its
director, Grotowski. His theater performed to great critical
acclaim in New York.

It is well worth your while to visit the National Museum of
Wroclaw, which has a unique collection of Silesian art. In
Poland where shrines to the Virgin Mary abound, Wroclaw is
the one town, perhaps the only town in western Europe, to
show a chubby smiling Virgin Mary, supporting a precocious
baby Jesus, standing on His Mother's knee with His right
hand touching his forehead as if he were greeting her. The
wooden sculpture dates from about 1360 and its official title is
"Madonna Enthroned on Lions." There are quite a few
madonna paintings and sculptures in that room. One dating
from about 1410 shows a really pretty smiling girl, also a
rendition of Mary.

The absolute "must see" treasure of Wroclaw, brought there
from Lwow, and recently restored by a gift from Lech Walesa
is the *Panorama of the Battle of Raclawice*. It is housed in a
rotunda and contains a single painting 15 meters high and 114
meters long, which wraps around the inside of the building.
It illustrates the battle of Raclawice fought and won by
Kosciuszko at the head of a peasant army in 1794. The Imperial Russian Army was defeated by a force inferior in number
and armaments, but evidently superior in spirit and leadership. The primary painters were Jan Styka and Wojciech
Kossak. Undoubtedly other painters added some detail under

instruction from the two artists. The painting is incredible because it gives the impression of great depth and the feeling of three-dimensionality. We felt as if we were walking through an actual battlefield. The painting was completed in less than one year.

We recommend that you fly from Warsaw to Wroclaw. It takes about an hour. Spend the day in Wroclaw and return to your Warsaw hotel in the evening. Be sure to have your reservations for the round trip. If you want to stay longer, the Hotel Wroclaw has good accommodations.

CHAPTER SEVENTEEN

The "Inner" Culture

Tourists are always invited to see the high culture of the country they visit. They look at imposing castles, sumptuous palaces, awe-inspiring cathedrals and spirit-enriching museums. And that is right and worthwhile, but we recommend that when you visit Poland you should try to get acquainted with the inner culture. By that we mean the life, the challenges and the fun, the chores, the work, the pleasures of extended families gathering to talk about the world and its problems as they see them, and as they understand how these great events will impact on their lives.

The door opener to this inner culture in Poland is the church. Most of us who go to church are in a hurry to get there and in a hurry to get out. We go to pray, we go to be seen and to see who else goes. We are usually quite generous when the collection plate is passed and we might even pay

attention to the sermon. But what would we do if the Sunday
ceremony of going to church was the "only show in town,"
the only real break in the monotony of very hard work dictated by the unchanging rhythm of seasons that we must
follow in order to survive. Sunday is the day when the peasants have the right to dress up, to go to church, to pray—yes,
but also to socialize in the church courtyard—if the weather
permits—to swap yarns, and gossip—and the Poles love to
gossip. The men eventually drift off to find a place to have a
drink; the boys do what boys do—ogle the girls dressed in
their Sunday finery—and the mothers try to guess if there is a
wedding in the offing. Life somehow slows down and is
reduced to its human size. There is a social fabric, a co-
hesiveness that is real and engulfs even the casual visitor. The
stereotype of the surly, harsh featured peasant, this mask we
are accustomed to seeing, is lifted. The weather-etched
creases are softened by smiles that radiate through the eyes,
are confirmed by parted lips which might show teeth, or a
toothless grin; after all, old men lose their teeth and somehow
survive without dentures, and no one thinks the less of them.
Old age has its rights, being toothless is one of them.

Every once in a while someone will rush off to their barn,
usually a kid somewhere between six and twelve years old,
boy or girl, it makes no difference. They have to do a chore;
even on Sundays the cows have to be fed and milked. Those
of us who live in cities and have cars know the slavery of
ownership. No matter how much we want to relax at home
and read our paper, we have to rush out to move the car from
one side of the street to another, because there is a sign that
tells us when we can not park in an area during certain hours
on certain days. The peasant equivalent of our servitude to
the car is his/her servitude to the cow. Its no fun to own a cow
and there is nothing romantic about milking one and cleaning
the stall. The cows do not know that it is Sunday. It helps to
have children, otherwise the woman of the house has the
chore. On holidays the men have the absolute right to be lazy.
What they must do is to go to church. If they choose not to,
they risk being excluded from the network of pleasure.

The Sunday ritual includes taking a bath in a tin tub placed in the kitchen and filled with scaling water that has been steaming on the large kitchen hearth. Then, the men shave, comb their hair and put on their Sunday/holiday clothes. Peasant men and women are not shy about wearing colorful costumes, richly embroidered, topped off with fancy hats and kerchiefs. The kids wear clean shirts, pressed pants, and shined shoes—these days they may wear sneakers, clean jeans and a colorful sweater.

Tourists rarely have the chance to participate, to enjoy the luxury of laziness. Yet they can do it and nothing we recommended in this entire book will give us greater pleasure than to tell you how to become part of this scene. It really is not difficult at all.

There are two ways of becoming part of that inner culture. It can be done on the grand scale: a feast with dancing and singing and more color and living art than can be found in even a fancy Broadway production. Then there is the small scale: more intimate, more conducive to making contact and more friendly. Both are centered on the church. To participate on the grand scale requires a visit to the chancery of the bishop in whose diocese you happen to be. If you are in Krakow, then you have to go to the cardinal's office and find out when he or his auxiliary bishop intend to make a visitation on one of the parishes in the diocese. It will always be on a Sunday or a special holiday. The secretary will be glad to tell you when and where this event will occur and ask you if you wish to go. If you do, he will not only tell you where to go and what the name of the parish priest is, he might even, without telling you, make arrangements that would enable you to have a good vantage point from which to see the ceremony, and to pray and, if you happen to be a Catholic, to receive communion from the bishop, or even the cardinal. Be sure to ask if the bishop intends to visit other parishes on dates more convenient to you. It will be to your advantage to make a specific arrangement.

You should get to the parish town on the Saturday, or even Friday, preceding the visitation. When you arrive, check in with the priest and he will make some arrangement for your lodging. You need not be too surprised if he had not made

these arrangements anticipating your arrival. If the priest
happens to be a monsignor, chances are very good that he
will have a room for you in the parish house and invite you to
dinner. The table will be set. The table cloth will be snow
white, the china quite delicate in design, the wine will be
excellent and so will be the dinner. You will be served by nuns
in immaculate white, traditional habits. You have to be ready
to accept the religious ceremony that precedes the dinner and
concludes it. If you are not a Catholic, you are expected to
stand quietly during the ceremony. Remember that you are
the honored guest, and not because of your status, but because there is an old Polish saying: "A guest in home—God in
the home." You need not worry that you do not speak Polish.
The priest will have invited someone from the village who
speaks some English, because he was in the U.S., or who
speaks excellent English, because he is a retiree of Polish
origin who returned to his native village. If you happen to
know just a few words in Polish, be sure to say them. You will
be appreciated, because you made the effort. And no matter
how you pronounce them, you will be complimented: "How
well you speak Polish." You owe your hosts the courtesy of
answering their questions without flattery, honestly and according to your convictions. They don't need propaganda,
and they are experts at recognizing propaganda when they
hear it. If they want to debate a question, go ahead. After all,
it is not every day that they can talk to a real "live" American.
Please, don't take pictures at dinner. You will have ample
opportunity to shoot more rolls of film than you anticipated.
Also, do not offer to pay for your accommodations. You can
show your gratitude when the collection plate is passed during the church ceremony.

Long before the bishop's arrival, the peasants from all
around the diocese will gather on the village green, a fancy
name for an open field. They will all be dressed in their finery
and gather in small groups. Each group will be from one
village or hamlet. You will be able to notice subtle variations in
their costumes. The smallest hamlet is proud of its identity
and often disdains the inhabitants from other hamlets and
their young men will not marry a girl from that place. If you

drove through these hamlets, you would be hard pressed to notice any difference.

The altar will be placed on a knoll, or on a raised platform. If the weather is uncertain, there will be a canopy to protect the altar, the bishop and the vestments, which are usually quite ornate.

Frequently, in one of the nearby villages there is a statue of a saint or of the Virgin Mary which is especially venerated. The villagers will carry the ikon to the Mass to be celebrated by the bishop. The sight of a dozen stalwart men in full regalia of the region, carrying the statue with great care to maintain its balance and with visible reverence and pride to have been chosen for the task, is reminiscent of the sacred illuminations found in medieval scrolls. The strength of faith is its unbroken continuity that makes the past present in today's events.

While you will probably not be introduced to the bishop, chances are he will smile and wave at you as he sits in the ornate armchair to the right of the altar. A Mass celebrated by a bishop is a very impressive ceremony, which includes a choir recruited from local talent. It is usually musically very good. Somehow devotional music sounds very real in an open area, surrounded by the gentle magnificence of a rural setting. This magnificence is usually invisible. It is not emphasized. But the ceremony, the colorful audience, the music, combine to bring out the majesty inherent in an old tree and lyricism present in a field of corn or the artistry suddenly visible in a row of haystacks.

The Mass itself is the same in a village field in Poland as it is in the ornate splendor of St. Peter's in Rome. In celebrating a Mass the bishop is not inferior to the Pope, for that matter neither is the village priest regardless of his rank in the Church hierarchy. The ceremony is impressive no matter what your beliefs are and even if you have none. One of the most interesting reactions of an old peasant woman who used to listen to the Mass was: "How come there is so much about the Jews in our religion?"

The Mass is always followed by a homily delivered by the bishop. Frequently the bishop will use the occasion to make a

statement of political significance. It will be a subtle statement, but understandable to the parishioners. One of the
subtlest statements made by a bishop at a time when Solidarity was an illegal organization occurred when he carried
the wooden cross around the altar. The front of the cross was
plain, but as the bishop turned to walk to the back of the altar,
the backside of the cross was clearly visible and burned into it
was the word "Solidarity" in the distinctive script used by the
illegal organization. When the government objected to the
bishop's engaging in political activities, his answer was quite
simple: "Solidarity is a basic tenent of our Church and the
artistry is part of the script—an old tradition." And that was
that. The cheers of the participants at the Mass echoed
through the fields and kept on echoing throughout Poland
until Solidarity became the legal power of democratic Poland.

This story illustrates the influence a bishop can have and
how carefully he uses it. Today he is likely to focus his homily
on some practical aspects of daily life under the now prevailing conditions. He will also certainly wait for the statue to be
brought to the altar and bless it. Bless the audience. Say a
short prayer. The choir will probably sing the ancient hymn of
Poland which proclaims the Virgin Mary to be the Queen of
Poland and then the bishop will leave. Usually he will go to
the parish house for a lunch and a little rest before departing.
The people will cheer him and then their own fun will begin.

And fun it is. Some groups will start singing their own
regional songs and spontaneously begin to dance. Others,
not unlike their unknown American cousins, will line up to
devour the superb homemade sausages and cakes and
cheeses, and sweets and anything else that can be eaten. It's a
fun orgy. It is also as certain as the sun rises in the East that
there will be vodka. Some of it will be official, and a lot of it
"the revenooers" never saw, and will be as potent as our own
"white lightning." If you happen to be in the southern part of
Poland, and we hope you are, there is a local plum vodka
sometimes known as "Slivovitz," but most frequently referred
to in Poland as "Peysahovka," which is 180 proof and superb.
Incidentally, the name "Peysahovka" is a Jewish name, because Jews who used to live in that region liked to drink it

during Passover (Pejsach). The Jews are gone, but the plum vodka is destined to remain as long as there are plums.

The dancing, eating, singing and drinking will go on until sundown. You will not be allowed to be just spectators taking pictures. Someone is sure to pull you in and once you become part of the festivities, you will stay because it's fun, it's real, and will forever be etched in your memory. There will be times when you are back home, perhaps barbecuing in your little backyard, when you will wish you could be back in that corner of Poland where you were not a tourist, just a someone having fun.

What we have just described was fun on the grand scale. Now there is a simpler small scale of seeing and participating in the non-tourist Poland, of gaining an insight into the inner culture. The door leading into it is the local village priest. Visit him on any Saturday and tell him you would like to come to church on Sunday and spend a Sunday afternoon in his hamlet (it is more fun in a hamlet of 170 houses and a small church than in a village which more than likely will be quite drab). We are certain that he will welcome you because the principle of "Guest in house. . . ." operates on all levels of Polish society. The Polish Pope had a seminar in his summer castle of Castel Gandolfo. One of the participants was Poland's leading philosopher Leszek Kolakowski, a confirmed atheist. The Pope knew of him and when he saw him he actually rushed over to greet him and said: "Guest in home. . . ." The people of the hamlet will feel the same way. This saying is actually the best description of Polish hospitality and you would have to have the exceptionally bad luck to find a boorish Polish family who would not want to have anything to do with you. The priest will find some family that can put you up, and it will probably be a family that either has someone who lives in the United States or someone who has been there. Walk around the hamlet for a while to give the family that will be your host for the night a chance to get ready for you, and then walk in to be greeted by smiling faces. Incidentally, the usual greeting when you walk into a peasant home is "Praised be Jesus Christ." The family will answer in a chorus "Forever and ever Amen." By greeting them in that way you acknowledge that you have a bond with them and that you wish them well. This is so important that we will write this greeting in Polish, but spell it phonetically. Try to remember it. Its a "magic" key to peasant Poland, to that inner culture. Here we go: "Nyek benje pokvalony Yesus Krystoos." Say it slowly and feel the warmth of your hosts for the night envelop you.

Depending on the well being of the hamlet and what the family is having for dinner, you might find yourself in luck and have pierogi filled with potatoes, or you might have just potatoes with sour milk (something like yogurt) and, as happened to us, you might have to eat it by spooning it (with a wooden spoon) out of a common bowl. You certainly will have tea and either a piece of delicious pound cake, or some other sweet. If you are offered sausage, or ham, while the family is eating their potatoes, don't refuse it, but cut thin slices and put them on your bread. If you really can't take the potatoes and sour milk, you can always eat the very tasty peasant bread, fresh butter, and usually a jam made from black berries or fresh honey. The honey will not have been filtered; the jar will be filled with beeswax containing the honey. You will be eating your breakfast for dinner, but one expects anything from Americans. The likelihood that you will have such a meager dinner is remote, especially on Saturday evening, but it is possible, because Sunday you will feast. The Sunday lunch menu is usually chicken soup with dumplings (very good and tasty) followed by the chicken. We are convinced that every Polish chicken must have been a long distant runner—all muscle and bone—and very little meat. The potatoes will be very tasty, and the vegetables will surprise you. Please remember not to drink the milk: you are not immune to what you may get from natural milk (straight from the cow, not pasteurized or homogenized), and you may get very ill if you do drink it. The water is safe to drink. So is the vodka.

Families usually go to the eleven o'clock Mass. They have too many chores to do to go earlier. Some go to the six o'clock Mass and do their chores later. Your hosts will go to the eleven o'clock. Be sure to pay them. Ten dollars will be a lot, but you can not give them any less. Take their pictures and not only promise to send them, but be sure you do.

If you are lucky the hamlet you chose may still have one of the old-fashioned simple wooden churches that used to dot the Polish countryside before the walls of fire ignited by World War II burned down most of the magnificent, intricately decorated churches. Those that survived are being replaced by the thousand new churches under construction. Most of those are monstrosities of massive concrete, oddly shaped in the name of modern art. You will certainly notice them as you travel through Poland.

No matter what the church in your hamlet looks like, the people worshiping in it have not changed. They will come, dressed in their Sunday finery, and hopefully most will wear their regional costumes, although some will come in ill-fitting Sunday civies. It struck us that those who wore their regional costumes looked dignified, secure and proud. And those in ordinary suits looked poor, out of place, and showed the wear and tear of their harsh lives. They did not even smile as easily or talk as openly as their splendidly attired neighbors.

Your hosts will introduce you and again you are liable to find someone who will speak at least a little English. All over the world the most attractive group are the children and they will come around to look, to smile at you, and try to talk to you. They love to pose for pictures. If you happen to have a Polaroid and give them a print, you will "make their day." If by some chance you were to return to the hamlet years later, a grown-up would rush up to you and proudly show you the picture. Obviously a treasure, well preserved, and memorable because it brought the outside world into their lives, filled to the brim with monotony.

What is striking is to see how those graceful, charming, delicately featured youngsters grow up to be rather heavy-set women and dull-faced men. You will notice it because you will see their parents. The harshness of life, the production of children, the days filled with chores, and the marriages to taciturn, somewhat brutish men who find their solace in drink, age women quickly and gracelessly. We talked to them about women's rights, about feminism, and they laughed at us—a little embarrassing—not because they did not under-stand us, but because in the context of their lives it made no sense. The young women listened, understood and told us that as soon as they grow up they intend to leave the hamlet to live and work in a city. The young men, while they dis-agreed with the budding feminism, also emphatically stated that they too will leave the village to work in the city. The escape of youth from the farms is a widespread phenomenon in Poland and causes despair for the parents, real problems for the government which needs the food produced by these tiny farms, and, tragically, works out very badly for the young people. City air no longer guarantees freedom. More often it guarantees poverty, bad jobs, and miserable lodgings as sub-tenants living in one room. Most of these expatriates from the land survive because their mothers send them food packages. It is a sorry tale, but well known to American city dwellers. The fatal attraction of the bright lights is the devilish magnet, the real drug attracting the young away from se-curity, comfort, status, to join the race after the proverbial brass ring. Some win, most degenerate into urban inhu-manity. But standing in front of the little church and looking at the bright faces so full of hope and joy of living, we felt like scrooges when we tried to rob them of their illusions. It would have been a useless exercise anyhow.

The chimes of the bell remind all that it is time to go to Mass. The inside of the church is usually decorated by sculp-tures of local artists. Their work has the charm and integrity of primitivism. You will notice the many candles in front of saints, each of whom has a special "function." He may protect the family, assure good harvests or help the sick; the candles are either a plea or an expression of gratitude. The dominant art is a stylized painting (usually artistically quite second rate) of the Virgin Mary. Her Son, if He is even present, is con-signed to a dark corner of the altar. The candles, the flowers and the prayers all flow to the Virgin Mother. The male chauvinism of the culture is parked at the church door.

The ceremony will be simple and if the young priest is still insecure, he will perform all the rituals by rote. The people will be lined up to receive communion and the service will conclude with the singing of a hymn. All of it will not take longer than perhaps half an hour. The priest, old or young, knows that his congregation wants to enjoy the one day of freedom from chores they have.

You might want to visit one of Poland's most important cultural institutions, the church school. It is clean and made cheerful by the children's art. It is a universal language understood because it is created by children throughout the world, an explosion of color and free flowing imagination. But what will be striking is the school's emphasis on Poland's culture and history. These two areas were really perverted by the communist regime. Now things will change, but the church school in the small villages all over Poland will continue to have a tremendous impact on the social conscience of the people of Poland. This is neither good nor bad; it is a fact.

When the church service is over, the real socializing begins. The women will stand in small groups and probably look you over to see if you wear make-up and glittering jewelry. This is their stereotype of the American woman. That is the way those among them who went to America look when they come back. The old women, in their late thirties, have beautiful skin, and natural coloring that no make-up can ever duplicate. Their beauty secret is the clean spring water used to scrub their faces, and the avoidance of all chemicals to enhance their beauty. They liked my wife because she wore "no paint." If they will envy anything about you, it will be the slim figure of most American women, and the clothes they wear. But if you happen to be chubby, they might like you even more.

The men will stand around, smoke their cigarettes and look at you and whomever you are with. They try to guess if you are rich and try to understand why on earth you came to their hamlet. You will be the subject of their conversation while you are among them and you will remain the subject of their conversation for a few Sundays to come. For them you are "the only show in town." If you find someone who speaks English, perhaps one of the kids is learning it, walk over and talk to him. They will overcome their shyness and bombard you with questions. Most of them will be curious about getting to America and finding work. They have heard about the new laws making it difficult to find work without the proper papers. They have heard that the President ordered that no visas are to be given to Poles. They will look to you to confirm these stories. If you do, because it is true, it will start an argument among the men, because they have heard that someone from the neighboring village did get a visa and is now working somewhere in New Jersey or Chicago, or Bridgeport. So how come you are saying that what they heard is not true? No matter what you say, it will cause a debate. America is such a dream for them that they hate to believe anything negative about this country. When they see on their TVs pictures of the homeless, they say "It's communist propaganda." Now they will say our government does not want us to leave because they need workers, so they are scaring us. Perhaps it is even true, but the homeless are blacks; white people get jobs. Racism is a fact of life among Polish peasants, and not only peasants.

The little groups will begin to go each to their respective destination. The women will go home to heat up the Sunday lunch, the kids will go off to their chores or to play, the men will go to have a few—and then join their families. The street will empty out. The priest will come to say good-by and invite you to come again. The hamlet's color will be gone and it will put on its every day face, melancholy and secure in its traditional unchangeability. You have just been a part of the small scale. Neither you nor the people of the hamlet will forget your visit to their version of the inner culture.

CHAPTER EIGHTEEN

Sporting Life

Before we tell you about the great opportunities existing in Poland for horseback riding, hunting, fishing, boating, skiing and iceboating, there is one participatory activity is that is unique, fun, and very healthy. And that is mowing hay.

If you happen to be in any of the agrarian sections of Poland in late spring or early fall, you will see great fields of grass, deep green and highlighted by wild flowers. They range from bright yellow to a very deep blue, colors associated with the best of Van Gogh's paintings. The fields will be dotted with groups of men, women and children, all smiling, chattering and singing while they mow the grass the old-fashioned way, with scythes. In a way their motions and progress through the fields looks like a stylized ballet. Every movement is rhythmic, careful, and the cut grass falls in neat rows. While most of the cutting is done by men, the raking of the grass with long handled wooden rakes is the chore of women and children. They gather the grass, still wet, into loose piles to be dried by the sun. Eventually, when the grass turns golden dry, it will be gathered into fancy haycocks. The shape of the cocks is a basic pyramid, with rounded sides and what appears to be a crown on top. Each region has a slightly different way of topping off the haycocks. They remain standing to dry out thoroughly to provide the fragrant fodder for the cows during the long winter days.

If you happen to drive by and are wearing appropriate clothing, you can stop the car, get out and walk over to the field. You can indicate that you too would like to join in. You can be certain that there will be a spare scythe and certainly a spare rake. Even if you never held a scythe in your hands, you will quickly learn how to aim at the bottom of the long helms of grass, and by watching the experienced peasants you will learn how to hold it and the rhythm of the motion will be dictated by the rhythm of the songs.

Ranking the grass is easier and actually more fun. You need not feel awkward if you happen to be a man doing the raking. The kids have a ball. They will rake for awhile and when they have a pile that looks deep enough, they will throw themselves on top. No one gets angry. The harmony of the work creates a sense of unity that buries, at least temporarily, the usual rivalries which criss-cross small communities.

You will be an added attraction, another dimension of the fun and you will be most welcome. You might be an excuse for some men to catch a little snooze under a tree and for the women to gossip at leisure. The work starts with sunrise and continues until sundown. The intensity is dictated by the fear of rain, the great enemy of harvest time. Every bit of sunshine has to be utilized to the maximum.

Around ten o'clock, there is a break. The men will unload from their horse-drawn carts jars of drinks and baskets of food. The drinks will be remarkably cool and very refreshing. Most of the drinks will be juices from berries diluted with spring water, some will be cold tea, and, yes, there will be stronger drinks. But comparatively little heavy drinking goes on. Alcohol and working in the sun do not mix. The food baskets are containers of unexpected delicacies, of superb, home baked bread, fresh sausage (half veal, half pork) wonderful cakes and cookies for the kids. All work stops and no food at any restaurant ever tasted so good and company was never more joyful. The talk will be about the grass, and how good it looks and full of the hope that it will dry well and the little calves will grow well and the cows will give a generous supply of milk.

You can stay as long as you want to. They will be sorry to see you leave and try to convince you to ride back with them for the evening meal. Don't be surprised if the men embrace you (the men in your party), and the women hug the women in your party. The kids will politely shake hands, but you can hug them. Somehow, for a little while, you belonged to them. Somehow you were part of nature, not as an observer, but as a welcome servant. Your muscles will probably be stiff, but not your soul. There is a strength and joy gained in an intimate relationship with living, colorful and quietly splendid nature which replenishes the sense of being human that will remain with you long after the hay has been consumed by the calves and the cows and the horses. Cutting the grass on your lawn to the harsh noises of your lawn mower is a chore, not so mowing grass.

Now, the time has come to leave the simple, sometimes crude, often seemingly naive world of the peasants, their joys, chores, hopes, and monotony and move to the splendid, luxurious, exclusive, world of thoroughbred horses and the aristocratic sport of riding.

Horseback Riding

In a country whose history is filled with stories of magnificent cavalry charges, it is only reasonable to expect that the horses will be purebred, magnificent to look at, and a joy to ride. These horses require great care, are expensive to maintain and thus have been the exclusive property of Poland's aristocracy. Historically, riding was the privilege of the rich and well born. In this one respect at least the best of Poland is remarkably similar to the best of England. No English lord was better mounted than his Polish counterpart. This is true not only of the horses, but also of all the equipage associated with the sport of riding from the elaborate saddles to the riding habits. All are available for purchase.

To participate and be able to take full advantage of the many centers for riding requires careful planning before your departure. You have to select the area where you want to ride, what kind of horses you want to ride and what kind of riding you would like to do. The principal riding centers are listed in the "Almanac for Tourists" in the second chapter of the guide.

Most of the centers are located in the western part of Poland. Our preferred center, however, is Janow Podlaski, located close to the Russian frontier, at the edge of the great national park we told you about. Janow Podlaski has magnificent Arabian horses, beautiful to look at, high spirited to ride and perhaps the noblest of the species. Incidentally, some of the horses sold at auction fetch up to a million dollars. The auctions at Janow Podlaski are usually held in mid-September.

The general rules of participation in the sport are: You have to agree to stay at least five days at the center and ride for at least one hour per day. You must have accident insurance purchased in Poland and a third-party insurance against damage caused while on horseback. Races and hunts are organized by the center for groups of a minimum of 15 people. There are charges for each hour of riding inside or outside the center and special charges for riding with an instructor and jumping. The accommodations range from excellent, luxurious to very adequate. The restaurants are usually first rate. This is true because most of the riding centers are located on the grounds of Poland's aristocracy which are well maintained even in the absence of their original owners.

Arrangements have to be made through the Orbis Polish Travel Bureau, 500 Fifth Avenue, New York, NY 10036 (212 391-0844). We recommend that you write to them, tell them when you intend to be in Poland, where you will spend most of your time, what kind of riding you would like to do and whether you will bring your own equipment or would like to rent/buy it in Poland. The equipment from saddle to boots is of very high quality. You will receive a detailed reply to your inquiry and colorful brochures to help you make your choice. Once you do decide you will have to send a non-refundable deposit. We can not give you the specifics because all prices in Poland are changing, all are increasing.

You can also make the arrangements through Animex main office in Warsaw. The exact address is Chalubinskiego Street 8, 00-613 Warsaw, Poland. Allow ten days for your letter to be delivered and about 14 days to receive an answer. Animex seems to be well organized and knowledgeable. Orbis has a better worldwide network of agencies. Orbis still has the monopoly on tourism in Poland and controls reservations in hotels. This monopoly might also be subject to change.

Hunting and Fishing

In a basically agrarian country where a scant three decades ago 70 percent of the population lived on and off the land, hunting and fishing were sheer delight. There are very few people in the entire world who believed Rachel Carson, who in 1963 wrote the chilling saga of a *Silent Spring,* one without music of chirping birds. She did not write this book in Poland, and she certainly did not have Poland in mind.

Poland was among the first to designate vast areas as national parks. Cutting down of trees was subject to stringent regulations and licensing requirements and nature was revered in literature and poetry. Yet it is in Poland where the prophesy of a silent spring is close, perilously close, to reality.

The lakes, the rivers, the seashore, the major cities are vast ecological disasters. Part of it can be blamed on the ravages of a terrible war, part of it can be blamed on the system, although the fact that the ecology was in danger was recognized by Poland's Communist regime. It initiated an intensive reforestation campaign and was helplessly conscious of the need to do more. The real culprit in Poland was the same as everywhere: industrialization oblivious of its ecological impact. The process was more pernicious in Poland than in other European countries because the state was obligated to fill production quotas imposed on it by the economic plans of Stalin. Prodded by him and partially prompted to it by the Polish Communist Party who desired spectacular achievements, industries grew like the proverbial mushrooms after the rain.

Unfortunately the rain became acid, and the industries whose products the Polish people needed were built, although Poland had to import the raw material needed by that industry. Moreover, the basic source of energy for that industry was and is still coal. And the export of coal, along with the electrical energy generated through the use of coal were, and continue to be, Poland's primary export commodities.

It does not matter who will govern Poland; it does not matter if Poland becomes a market-driven economy. The primary task is to begin an intensive program of restoring the ecology.

The Chernobyl disaster came close to pushing whole areas of Poland over the brink and condemning them to infertility for centuries. Fortunately the atomic fall-out was contained, but Poland has to pay its $40 billion debt no matter what further damage this will do to the ecology. When it comes to money owed to Western banks, ecological factors are of no concern. If there is such a phenomenon as a political conscience, the rich countries, the lenders must voluntarily take the back seat to the demands of ecologically sound economic development not only in Poland, but all over the world.

It is still possible to hunt and fish in Poland, but both activities are strictly regulated and the regulations are enforced.

All hunting arrangements have to be made through the Orbis Hunting Bureau, Intraco Bldg, 2 Stawki Street 00-193 Warsaw, prior to your departure. These arrangements can be made by your travel agent or by you directly. Hunting is quite expensive. An overnight stay at the luxurious hunting lodges including all meals costs $150 per person, or $170 for a couple. All other accommodations, less than deluxe, cost $70 to $90 for a couple. There are registration fees and fees per shoot. The fee depends on what game you are hunting. In addition, you have to pay the official hunter who accompanies you, and beaters must be hired if required. If you do not speak Polish, there is a fee for an interpreter. There is a great variety of game that can be hunted. There are specific dates when a species can be hunted. These dates can be obtained from the Orbis Hunting Bureau. The ranges of animals goes from bisons to rabbits, from wild boar to deer and partridge.

You can bring your own hunting rifle and ammunition. Both must be declared to customs upon entering and shown to customs upon leaving. If your gun is lost, stolen, or accidentally destroyed, this has to be immediately reported to the police and the police have to give you the appropriate statement you will have to show when leaving.

For us, the greatest fun of hunting comes after the hunt or occurs even if there was no hunt. It is the most typical and traditional of Polish happenings, not related to Catholic or national holidays. It is the Kulig (pronounced "Cooleeg").

This is the place to spin a yarn of the "olden days" when ladies of good breeding and gentlemen of good stature, wrapped in gorgeous furs of mink and sable, and even ermine, assembled in the residence of a well-known member of the *szlachta* and decided to go on a Kulig. The countryside was bedecked by 12 feet of snow, the air was calm and the silvery moon was a powerful lantern illuminating the gently rolling hills casting a foreboding look on the distant forest. The blinking stars rivaled the diamonds gracing the necks of the well-born ladies and the graceful trio of horses pranced in anticipation of a chase, only slightly handicapped by the sleighs they would pull. Voices carry far in a cold night and the loud yelps of dogs and shouts of the beaters working the forest proclaim that they have discovered a wolf pack. It is time to go. Each beautifully ornamented sleigh accommodates, in addition to the driver, four guests. Most of the men are armed with rifles. On command, all the sleighs take off in a mad race across the fields, and since every lead horse has a distinctive sounding bell, the scene becomes a unique symphony of a chorus of bells, loud laughter, ribald songs yelled in a boisterous cacophony to the silent heavens.

It is well-known that wolves have greenish-yellow eyes that the moon and the snow cause to shine in a foreboding challenge. Suddenly a lead sleigh stops and the gentlemen shoot at the blackness between the eyes of their otherwise invisible prey. The beaters sound a horn when the shot hits the targets. There was a kill. A reason to celebrate. It is time to turn around and race back to the mansion, where whole piglets, roasted to perfection, await the "mighty" hunters.

The story has it that one hunter shot at a one-eyed wolf who was gray with age and honored by legend. The truth is at times an unwelcome intrusion of reality. The beaters brought the kill to the mansion, an autopsy showed that the wolf they brought was killed by a beater using an old fashioned front loading gun and not by a shot from the perfect English weapon, the proud possession of "the hunter." Since this particular truth was not allowed to intrude on the "reality" of the party, the fun was on.

The banquet would last for hours. The well-born ladies would graciously retreat to their chambers, while the gentlemen continued to consume amazing amounts of meat, and sausage, washed down with wines and vodka.

Those were the days, but . . . you can still enjoy a Kulig provided by the tradition-loving peasants and mountaineers. Our *fin de siècle* Kulig is now a joyful hayride with a group of happy tourists anticipating a fireside dinner of mutton sausage and Polish vodka. This type of Kulig can be arranged in the summer or winter and is really careless fun. The scenery will be the same, the songs of the peasants will be of the "olden times." The carriages will be the peasant wagons that haul manure, as well as hay. For the Kulig, however, the wagon will have fresh hay and the horses will wear the silver-adorned harnesses, the driver will don the colorful costume of the region and since you were not around in the "olden days," you will thoroughly enjoy a Kulig.

You can make the arrangements through your hotel or the Orbis bureau. The best Kuligs take place in the foothills of southern Poland, in the area we suggested you visit.

Fishing is just the thing to do after the noisy fun of the Kulig. Actually if you participated in a Kulig in southern Poland, chances are that you will find a mountain stream where you try your luck at handing a Glowacica, a rare species of fish which could weigh as much as 40 pounds. But it is sad to have to report that trout and salmon fishing are prohibited in all areas of Poland. Again the disastrous disregard for the environment makes itself painfully visible. In the past, just a few decades ago, Poland's rivers were a fisherman's dream. Whether you liked the leisurely fishing from a river's bank, or the more ambitious forms of fishing in or near rapids, you were certain to enjoy your own fish fry.

Today the last good fishing area to be found in Poland is the Mazurian Lakes, located in the northeastern regions of Poland, whose natural beauty we have described. The great lakes of Mamry, Dargin, Drweckie, and Szelak Wielki, (pronounced "Mamree," "Darkin," "Drvetskee," and "Shelok Vyelky") are the best lakes. Orbis maintains two excellently equipped fishing centers in Wilkasy (pronounced "Vilkasy") and Harsz (pronounced "Harsh"), which also offer sleeping accommodations. The varieties of fish are pike, bass, bream, roach and eel. The pleasure of fishing is the flexibility this sport affords. You can make it as strenuous or lazy as you want. Moreover, while you fish, your family can engage in one of our favorite pastimes, which is searching for mushrooms. The woods surrounding the lakes are the treasure house of Poland's world famous mushrooms. Their taste is incomparable and can they can be cooked in a campfire. A fresh fish fry with mushrooms is a mouthwatering dish. Be sure to bring wine or beer, or even the good standby, vodka. You can keep them cool by simply storing them in the cold water at the banks of the lake. For those who are confirmed urbanites, Orbis maintains very pleasant coffee houses with outdoor seating. If there is only one fisherman in your family and the others would like to do something else, there are places nearby where you can rent riding horses, and if that is too much, there are beautiful trails on which you can walk, think, and dream in peace and in the marvelous company of old trees. We remind you again to have a bug repellent with you.

Our favorite way to enjoy all of these activities is to rent camping equipment and find our own spot. The peace and quiet, the good air and the complete absence of time, the century, and problems, make us forget the mental and psychological baggage we seem to carry around because we have to. There is nothing that you have to do once you get to your spot. No matter where you go on a vacation, you reach a point where you don't want a fancy meal, you are tired of yet another museum or cathedral or palace, you are filled to the brim with tourism—that is the time to go to the Mazurian Lakes.

But it seems that the dedicated fishers are perhaps the most competitive group of people on earth. The world championships for flycasting were held in the picturesque San River of southern Poland. Perhaps you will catch a lot of fish, perhaps you will only come back with a magnificent fish story. It does not matter because you will enjoy the natural beauty that surrounds you. The best time for fishing in Poland are the months of August, September, October—a time frame which happens to correspond the the fabulous weather of the Polish autumn. There are rules and regulations governing the size of the fish and the type of bait you can use, and you also need a fishing permit. The helpful Orbis personnel will take care of all formalities and tell you where the fish are biting. Make your arrangements at the hotel in advance of your fishing expedition. If you did take our advice and got a car and a driver you can forget all the formalities. The driver, most likely also a fisherman, will know where that one real place for fishing can be found, and he will not only take care of the few formalities, he will also bring all the equipment and if you do not object, will bring his wife or son along. Fishing and hunting for mushrooms are a favorite occupation of urban Poles because they can bring back food not easily found in stores. American tourists must remember that U.S. Customs do not permit the importation of food. Sorry, but you cannot bring the superb dried mushrooms with you; you have to buy them in a specialty delicatessen in your home town and pay the high price for a delicacy nearly all Poles can afford.

Winter Sports

For most of us, Poland seems too far away to spend a week skiing. But is it really? There are 800 miles of mountain ranges with thousands of places suitable for skiing. There are about 390 ski lifts in operation and hundreds of marked ski trails. The best time to go skiing in Poland is from the middle of February to the end of March. You can get the most reliable information from the Polish Tourist Information Center we previously mentioned. Skiing in Poland is still a real sport requiring the stamina of an outdoors lover willing to accept simple accommodations, friendly companions, and a little adventure. The rich and famous will be in Gstaad or Zurs or St. Moritz showing off their well fitting and revealing skiing outfits. In Poland anything suitable for skiing is just fine. Skiing is not a fashion show; it is also not an invitation to display a sprained ankle. You don't have to show off that you have mastered the slalom, or know how to schuss down a steep slope in record time. You can ski at your level and enjoy the sun and the snow and get a tan that rivals any brought back by the rich and famous. In the game of one-up-manship, going skiing in the politically most exciting country in the contemporary world is quite an ace in the hole. Seriously though, a winter vacation in Poland is exciting and very affordable, and eight hours flying time from New York City's JFK.

Boating

We left for the end of the guide a sport that requires stamina, courage, and real know-how—that is kayaking. Poland's mountain streams, especially those that cascade down from the Carpathian Mountains, offer a real challenge to those who like shooting rapids and navigating rivers through narrow gorges. Those who are in the know realize the excitement and the beauty of seeing forests and mountains from the perspective of a river. Their majesty and color take on a grandeur and splendor not visible from any other vantage point.

You also have the option of floating down the lazy streams of Poland's great rivers: the San, the Bug and the Vistula. Especially rewarding is a trip down the San and the Bug which traverse southern and part of central Poland. Only a lyrical poet can describe the sights, the colors, and the gentle melancholy of the vistas that will unfold for you. Actually it is worth your while to go to Poland, stay a few days in Warsaw and Krakow and then get your kayak and float through Poland's land and history. Freed of the noise of cities, cars, and the din of all modern life, you can feel what living is, perhaps what it was meant to be. You can think, you can confront yourself, you can let your imagination roam, or you can just watch the river flow. We lost the sense of time and there was no one to tell us that we must pay attention to time, that we must be somewhere on time. The setting sun told us that it was time to find a place to rest. If you have a little tent, you can find a spot on the river bank, pitch your tent or sleep in your sleeping bag under the sky. You are safe. The sun will also be your alarm clock and the chirping birds will remind you that it is time to get up. If you are used to boating, you will have your supplies. If you don't, the river will take you to a village where you will find what you may need. The Tourist Office in Warsaw, or the Orbis office in New York will be able to give you the specific information on how to arrange a "river view vacation." Again we remind you that all sporting trips require planning. If you don't plan and decide to improvise, you risk a nightmare instead of fun.

If you happen to be an enthusiast of iceboating, you can do it on the Mazurian Lakes. The world championships of that sport were held on these lakes in 1976 and they are a favorite with Swedish and German devotees. You will be in the company of experts, friendly experts to be sure.

CHAPTER NINETEEN

Epilogue

We could find no better way to end our "Companion Guide" than with a translation of the Christmas and New Years homily delivered by His Eminence Joseph Cardinal Glemp which he so graciously sent us as a Christmas greeting. It captures the spirit of Poland in a way we could never do it.

"Sisters and Brothers!"

1. In Between "The Inn" and "The Manger"

The birth of Jesus in the Bethlehem manger is for us not only a reason to be deeply moved but also [a cause] for profound wonder. First [let us reflect] on [our] being moved; it is improbable that the tiny Child laying on hay, enveloped by the tender care of the Mother and Saint Joseph, the Protector, would not evoke in us the feeling of pity and compassion, especially when we become aware Who this Child is, what future was communicated to His Mother even before He was born, especially that "God Almighty will give Him the throne of His forebearer David. . . . and that there will be no end to His rule." (Lk. 1: 32–33). The birth in the manger gives cause also to wonder. I want to bring to [your] attention the moral distance that arose between the Inn, at whose door the holy Family knocked before the birth of the Child and the Manger, a place to shelter animals who are outside the city limits— where the Savior was born.

The inn represents the official structures. Guests come, pay and are protected. They can meet other guests, exchange views, receive information. The inn has trained personnel, [maintains] food supplies, maintains accounts of expenses and profits, could be subject to control, make purchases and their requests are respected.

The manger is quite different. As the matter of fact there is no relationship between the Manger and the Inn. The Manger lives a separate life. The shepherds are interested in the grazing land, the security of the sheep, the sale of wool. The contact with the Inn is casual, occasioned by purchases and sales. Moreover life in the Manger flows according to a different rhythm and in a different dimension.

The relocation of Maria and Joseph from the Inn, where there was no room for the poor pilgrims from Nazareth, to the Manger in the field was a move to another dimension of social life. It could be said: it was an entry into the second level in which one hears orders from Angels and their songs, and happiness and the desire to help is awakened among the shepherds. Jesus will remain in that second level, in that area till the end of his life. The first attempt to establish contact with official circles represented by Herod could have a tragic end for the little Child. The second contact Christ had with the life of the official structures in reality had a tragic ending—His death on the Cross. From His place in the Manger Jesus Christ was registered in the census of the inhabitants of the Roman Empire. His next registration consisted of entering His name on a table in three languages which was placed on the cross, above the head of the Condemned saying: "Jesus of Nazareth, King of the Jews" (J.19:19)

2. Between the "Home" and "Homelessness"

In transforming the relationship "Inn—Manger" to contemporary times, we note that it is not enough to compare the "Marriott hotel with a sublease of an apartment in the garret of a building." Social life has become much more complex. During the Silvester Evening [New Year's Eve] thousands of people will have fun and plenty and console themselves that a part of the profits will go to the poor. To the poor—that means to whom? For drug addicts, for those left in solitude, for those who come for free meals? Many among the poor will find a way—despite their official status of poverty—to enjoy on their own the "Silvester." There are children's homes, homes for social refuge, jails, hospitals and other institutions in which a person can fell the solitude. All of them are included in some way by social concerns, occasionally modest and too modest. There are people left over about whose poverty even their neighbors know nothing.

On the 12 of November of the current year, the Holy Father proclaimed the Sainthood of Brother Albert—Adam Chmielowski. This new Saint is a challenge to our times. A hundred years ago in Krakow he began to extricate himself from the Inn to the Manger, from the drawing rooms to the warming rooms of the destitute. He entered the area of poverty, that lived the separate life of people from another world. Brother Albert reregistered into this other world, the world of people who did not only need hand-outs, but the entire man. He became the "Brother of our God." Today we have the actual, pressing problem, how to reach and make close to us the separated areas of villas, blocks of apartments and rooms shared by a few families. In reality, many people have an address, but do not have the warmth of a home.

3. To Notice the Emerging Good

It would be unfair if we expressed our appraisal of reality as we find it during Christmas 1989, only by complaints. For the picture to be more accurate, it is necessary not only to notice the desire of people trying to get closer one to the other, those from the evangelical Inn to those from the Manger, but to [record] the fact of the accomplished good.

Let us think of these hands from opposing camps stretching out to exchange a hug. In the changes occurring in the world we perceive signs which predict the breaking of barriers separating closed areas. The Polish Prime Minister exchanges handshakes in Moscow and it's not just a routine gesture. It is the liturgical sign of peace extended to the Chancellor of the German Federal Republic and it is not a routine gesture, but a deeply human one. In the Vatican the Author of "perestroyka" shook the hand of the Pope, the Author of the encyclical "Solicitudo Rei Socialis," and the world understands that "in spite of the sad experiences of the years . . . the Church must emphatically confirm, that it is possible to vanquish obstacles" (SRS, 47).

In the beginning of this year we experienced that the hand shakes at the round table, supported by will and—frequently—prayer brought the desired changes. It is necessary therefore to hold out hands for a friendly shake. Lots of people wait for a handshake.

We are not lacking wealthy people who would like to help the poor. Still we frequently lack the means which would credibly mediate between the giver and the receiver. It is necessary therefore to revitalise the charitable activities in the parishes. It is necessary to increase the ranks of volunteers to find at first the people who are really in need. We can not wait for them to announce their existence. Charitable associations should thoroughly and responsibly go to every corner of a Parish and with love find those who await a contact with a well meaning human being. . . .

Invite to the Christmas table those who can not afford to prepare an ordinary holiday meal. Let this year the traditional chair that is left empty be occupied.

—Josef Card. Glemp
—Prymas Polski

Warsaw, Christmas 1989 A.D.

Appendix: Reflections on the Capital of "New Freedom"

History leaves deep scars and indelible memories even among those who do not know their history. Americans are a good example of that truth. For the younger generation even the assassination of JFK is a distant event, and not much more than a movie spectacle. Many Poles do not know their history, or know the "false" history written by Poland's perpetual enemies—the Russians, both Czarist or Bolshevik, and the Germans, both Prussian or Nazi.

Warsaw is a perfect example of the tremendous contradictions and falsifications of Poland's history. Even at this moment when the Poles are truly enjoying freedom of the press, freedom of assembly and freedom of conscience, history is used as a political weapon. History is used as a beacon to ferret out scapegoats—those responsible for all the tragedies that befell the people of Poland. History, like the Bible, can be quoted by scoundrels and saints alike. The listener has the right to choose whom he or she believes. Swastika graffiti is visible on some walls. Some say that all the tragedies of Poland were brought on by the Jews. There is a rumor that most of the current Polish government is controlled by Jews. The statistical fact that there are fewer than 10,000 Jews left in Poland does not matter to the advocates of anti-Semitism.

They claim that the "others," whoever they are, are crypto-Jews with Polish sounding names.

This tragic misuse of history will have dire effects in most of the nations emerging from the ruins of the "evil empire." For example, no one disputes that the Ukrainian people have the right to create their own state, but there never was a Ukrainian nation. That republic is an entirely new creation which is yet to write its own history. But, for no good or valid reason, the Ukrainian nationalists are desperately searching for some distant historical roots which would allow them to lay claim to some slice of Poland that does not belong to them, or claim that a city was for centuries the capital of their cultural existence.

Recently, a letter written to the editor of the New York *Times* claimed that the city of Lviv was always the center of Western Ukrainian culture. The historical Polish name of the city was Lwow. The city was dignified by a royal decree of a Polish king to be a "Royal City." That was as far back as the 17th century. Lwow had a Polish university, a magnificent theater where all the plays were performed in Polish. Moreover, Lwow was singularly liberal, encompassing a large Roman Catholic Armenian, Jewish, and Uniate (Greek Orthodox, but accepting the Pope of Rome as its head) community. Lwow was perhaps the only city in Europe which was the home of three great religions.

The letter to the editor went so far as to claim that there was even a museum of Ukrainian culture. The contents of the museum included folk art and an empty bottle of vodka with the label "Zid" on it—the pejorative name given to Jews, many of whom did run taverns.

This little aside written with malice towards none is however a trumpet sounding a warning: nationalism can be fanned into a roaring fire and that fire will not be restricted to distant Azerbijian, or some far off Islamic land, but may quickly break out in all of free Eastern Europe and consume that freedom very quickly. Neither Russia nor Germany will stand for it. And historically Russia and Prussia/Germany kept peace in that part of the world, a peace that was at times restrictive, but at times beneficial to the people and the economy.

While you as a tourist are in the midst of freedom and enjoying the sights and sounds of that freedom, you are also in the middle of a cauldron of historical forces on the brink of boiling over.

This information is given in a guide for tourists, some of whom may be business people, some may be potential students, and some may even undertake the thankless task of acting as consultants to steer institutions through quicksand.

Those among you who are tourists or have long term plans to become involved in some aspect of Poland's development will become aware that there is a perpetual tension in the air among intellectuals, politicians, artists and just plain folk. The "shock treatment" of a free market economy following decades of drab socialist security is truly a spiritual blessing, but with portents of economic disaster.

Although the word "spiritual" is basically a theological concept, it has very realistic consequences in a country whose people embark on a course of "freedom of choice," a freedom not based on official sanction or curbed by the limits of an ideology. It is very difficult for anyone to make a choice without a compass telling him what is "right" or "wrong." An ever increasing number of Poles are beginning to make the right choices. They do not chase the "easy, quick buck," but are evolving into serious business people. They are learning the complexities of trade, the structures of economic integrity, and the limits of their individual potential.

The dismemberment of the Soviet Union is, however, again creating an economic turmoil in Poland. The Lithuanians, Ukrainians, Russians, etc., are now beginning to go through the "quick buck" phase of their freedom and are increasingly turning toward the Poles who have—comparatively speaking—greater experience, to act for them as middle men in trade with the West. The Polish entrepreneurs have become the commodity brokers for the newly emerging east European nations. Poland, as an independent kingdom, as a province of Imperial Russia, Germany and Austria, was always the highway for West-East trade, investments and industrial development. This long historical tradition is overlooked by the head-long rush of business people directly to Russia or the Ukraine. The Poles know how to work with the other Eastern nations. The Germans and Austrians are well aware of this fact and thus have the highest economic profile in Poland and use the Polish "know-how" to their advantage. Americans have to overcome their stereotypical notion of Poles and the only way they will overcome it is by visiting the country.

This aside cuts into the spiritual aspects of freedom. In the context of this book, this theme is not philosophy but hard reality. The Roman Catholic Church is the guardian of the spiritual aspects of Poland's freedom. Having made it possible for Solidarity to win, the Church has become a real political power. While the hierarchy will deny that it has a political agenda, because the Church is not supposed to have one, it does, especially a Church guided by a "Polish pope." The fascinating aspect of the Catholic political agenda is that just as it opposed materialism in its Communist version, it opposes materialism (consumerism) in its capitalist version. The Church wants to implement a program of Christian democracy, a program which includes a very high degree of sensitivity to the needs of the poor, disadvantaged, elderly population. The real, substantive political dialogue in Poland is between the passionately secular intelligentsia and the moral strictures inherent in any church sponsored political program. In the long history of Poland the government, and especially the ruling elite of Poland, seldom knuckled under to the demands of the Church. The Pope is obviously aware of this and has given strict directives to the Church to keep out of politics and stick to the basic functions of the Church. The entire future of the very delicate Polish experience in democracy depends on an accommodation between the vision of the Poland's church and Poland's secular politics.

These political reflections are an absolute necessity to understand the soul of one of the most political capitals of Europe—political not in the sense of Washington politics, but in the sense of the politics of a nation's survival.

Index

alcoholic beverages, 67, 76, 91, 109–110, 150
Aleje Ujazdowskie, 54–55
Alexander I, 45, 46
amber, 109
American Embassy, 54, 133, 134–135
architecture, 56–57, 67, 69, 96, 109, 112
art, 77–79, 123–129, 142; see also shopping
artists, 131–135
Augustynow Forest, 121
Austria, 35, 43, 45, 96; see also Habsburg Empire
Austrio-Hungarian Empire, 89–90

Baltic Sea, 107
battle of Grunwald, 117–118
Belweder, 54–55
Bialowieza National Park, 67
Bialystok, 67
Bieszczady region, 95
Bismark, Otto von, 139
boating, 167–168
Breslau see Wroclaw
buses, 16, 17

Canaletto, 31, 40
car rentals, 17–18, 67
castles, 32, 33–37, 52, 72, 73, 117
Cathedral of Gniezno, 104–105
Chopin, Frederick, 49, 64
churches, 47, 48–49, 53, 76–77, 95, 96, 103, 104, 111, 153
Church of the Holy Cross, 48–49
Clothiers Market, 74
coffee houses, 44, 55, 165
Collegium Maius, 79
Congress Kingdom, 45–46
Constitution of the Third of May, 35
Copernicus, 72, 117
credit cards, 19
Crusaders, 100–101
cuisine, 14, 50–51
culture, 21–25, 74, 89; defense of, 43–44; "inner," 145–146
currency, 12, 75; exchange, 12–13, 94–95
Czartoryski Palace, 78

day trips, 61–69
Dolina Chocholowska, 87
drivers, 16, 84, 109
Duchy of Warsaw, 45
"Dziady," 43–44

film industry, 133–134
fishing and hunting, 161–166
food, 14–15, 50–51, 69, 85, 91, 152, 166; see also alcoholic beverages; cuisine
furniture, 112–113, 124, 125, 127–129

Galicia, 89, 91
Gdansk, 24, 39, 40, 65, 107–113, 118; churches, 14; during WWII, 109, 113; furniture, 112–113; history, 107–109, 110–112; hotels, 15, 109; restaurants, 109
Geysztor, 34
Ghetto Monument, 32
Ghetto Uprising, 28, 32, 35–36, 41, 57
Glemp, Joseph (Cardinal), homily of, 169–172
Gniezno, 99–105

Habsburg Empire, 43, 51
hamlets see peasants
hetman, 36
Hitler, Adolph, 39, 49, 80, 109, 115, 118, 141
Hohenzollern, Albrecht, 77–78
Hohenzollerns, 118
Holocaust, 57, 58
Holy Roman Empire, 22, 23, 100
horseback riding, 159–161
hotels, 15, 50, 53, 84, 92, 96, 97, 109, 113, 120, 139
Huculs, 95
hunting and fishing, 161–166

Jagiellonian University, 72, 78–79, 134
Jewish Cemetery, 57
Jews, 24, 31–32, 57, 59, 67, 90, 100, 141, 149, 150–151

John Paul II (Pope), 73, 74, 77, 80,
    93, 97, 101, 102–103, 104

Kampinos Jungle, 62–64
Kasprowy Hotel, 84, 87
Kiepura, Jan, 92
Knights of the Cross, 117–118
Kolbe, Maximilian, 103; Mass of
    canonization of, 103–104
Kosciuszko, Tadeusz, 49, 78
Krakow, 24, 30, 33, 39, 45, 64, 71–
    81, 147; churches, 76–77; history,
    76–78; hotels, 15; museums, 77–
    79; region surrounding, 79–80;
    restaurants, 73, 75–76; shopping,
    74–75, 77, 125
Kulig, 163–164

language, defense of, 43–44;
    learning, 19–20, 134
Lazienkowski Gardens and Palace,
    54
Lenin, Vladimir, 43, 78
Lesko, 95
LOT Airlines, 12, 17
Lowicz, 64–65
Lublin, 96, 97
Lwow, 141

magnates, 23, 24, 25, 96–97
Majdanski, Kazimierz, 81, 103
Matejko, Jan, 77, 78
Mazurian Lakes, 120–121, 165, 166,
    168
Mickiewicz, Adam, 42, 43–44, 49
Mieszko I (King), 99–100
Mieszko II (King), 100
"Miracle on the Vistula," 40–41
monasteries, 48, 80–81
Monastery of Jasna Gora, 80–81
monument of Mickiewicz, 43, 44
monument of Poniatowski, 45, 49
mountain people, 86–87
museums, 59–60, 64, 77–79, 120–
    121, 139–140, 142
Mustafa, Kara, 51–52

Napoleon, 35, 45, 46
national anthems, 46, 48
National Museum, 31, 64
Nazi Germany, 28, 30, 35–36, 41, 49,
    54, 57, 58–59, 64, 65, 87, 139, 141
Nowa Huta, 72

Old Town Market, 31–32, 125
Orbis, 11–12, 15, 97, 98, 120, 132,
    160, 161, 162, 163, 164, 165, 166,
    168
Ottoman Empire, 51–52, 118, 119,
    138

Palace of Culture, 55–56
palaces, 32, 33–37, 51, 54–56, 64,
    96–97
Palace Square, 39, 40, 42
Panorama of the Battle of Baclawice,
    142–143
parks, 67, 137–138
peasants, 23–24, 45, 68–69, 74, 90,
    91, 124, 145–156; art, 124–125;
    church life, 146–150, 151–152,
    153, 154–155; country, 89–98;
    festivals, 150–151; gatherings, 91;
    hamlets, 146–156; homes, 84–86,
    91, 121, 147–148, 151–153; "inner"
    culture, 146–156; work of, 157–
    159
Pilsudski, Jozef, 40
Poland, and German boundaries,
    80–81; and Roman Catholic
    Church, 59, 99–105; during
    WWII, 27–30, 39, 41, 49–50, 54,
    58–59, 65, 109, 113, 118, 141;
    eastern, 115–121; economy, 12,
    13, 68, 75; environmental
    problems, 162–163, 165;
    government, 25, 35–37, 45–46, 68,
    90, 110–111; history, 27–32, 33–
    37, 39–46, 47–52, 71, 76–78, 99–
    105, 107–109, 110–112, 116–119,
    138, 139, 140–142; "inner" culture,
    145–156; internal conflicts, 111;
    living in, 131–135; mountain
    regions, 83–87, 89–98; northern,
    99–105; partitions of, 35, 46, 108–
    109; regions of, regained after
    WWII, 119; 141; southern, 83–87,
    89–98; symbols of, 47–48; wars
    and conflicts with Russia, 40–41,
    43, 45–46, 59, 78, 96, 101, 118; war
    with Ottoman Empire, 51–52
Polish Communist Government, 43–
    44, 161–162
Polish Freedom Fighters, 28, 41, 54
Polish Patriotic Home Army, 28, 41,
    54
politics, 25, 35–37, 93–94

Poniatowski, Josef, 44, 45, 46
Poniatowski, Stanislaw August, 35
Powazki Cemetery, 57
powiat, 92–93, 94; market day, 94–95
Poznan, 24, 137–139; German presence in, 139; history, 139; hotels, 15, 139; museums, 139–140
Praga, 57–58
Prussia, 35, 43, 45, 100, 118
Przemysl, 91–92, 95–96; hotels, 96

recreation, 16, 65, 119–121, 157–168
Red Army, 41, 57, 65, 141
restaurants, 14–15, 50–51, 55, 73, 75, 109, 160
Revolutions of 1848, 42–43
Roman Catholic Church, 22–23, 24, 59, 99–105; Mass, 149–150, 152, 154–155
Royal Castle, 32, 33–37, 52
Russia, 45; rulership of Poland, 45–46; wars and conflicts with Poland, 40–41, 43, 45–46, 59, 78, 96; *see also* Soviet Union

"Second Miracle on the Vistula," 42
Sforza, Bona (Queen), 97
shopping, 13–14, 57–58, 68, 74–75, 77, 94–95, 112–113, 125, 127, 140
Sobieski, Jan, 50, 51–52
Sobieski, Marysienka, 51–52
social structure, 23–25
Solidarity, 37, 39–40, 48, 65, 73, 90, 93, 101, 102, 103–104, 108, 111, 150
Somosierra Pass, 45, 46
Soviet Union, 28, 34, 35; *see also* Russia
SPATIF, 55
sporting life, 16, 65, 157–168
Stalin, Joseph, 27–28, 41, 43, 55, 59, 78, 161–162
Stwosz, Wit, 76, 77
Sukiennice, 77, 125
Szczecin, 108–109
szlachta, 23, 24, 25, 36–37, 43, 45, 46, 101

Tatra Mountains, 30, 83–84; homes in, 84–86; hotels, 84
taxi, 16

Teutonic Knights *see* Knights of the Cross
trains, 16–17
transportation, 12, 15–18, 67
travel information, 11–20, 131–132; currency exchange, 12–13, 94–95; packing necessities, 18–19; transportation, 12, 15–18, 132

University of Warsaw, 49

Victoria Intercontinental, 50
Vienna, 51–52
visas, 12
Vistula River, 39, 40, 41, 42, 107
Virgin Mary, 48, 68, 80, 81, 142, 150, 154

Walesa, Lech, 42, 73, 142
Warsaw, 16, 24, 27–60, 118; architecture, 56–57; cemeteries, 57; churches, 47, 48–49, 53; coffee houses, 44, 55; day trips from, 61–69; during war with Bolshevik Russia, 40–41; during WWII, 27–30, 39, 41, 49–50, 54; embassies, 54, 55; gardens, 54; history, 27–32, 33–37, 39–46, 47–52; hotels, 15, 53; monuments, 42–46; museums, 59–60; palaces, 32, 33–37, 51, 54–56; restaurants, 50–51, 55; shopping, 57–58, 125; streets, 53–54; touring, 53–60; Uprising, 28, 32, 35–36, 41
Wawel Castle, 72, 73
Wieliczka Salt Mine, 79–80
Wierzynek, 75–76
Wilanow Palace, 50, 51
Winged Hussars, 52
winter sports, 166–167
World War I, 96, 109
World War II, 27–30, 39, 41, 49–50, 54, 58–59, 65, 109, 113, 118, 141
Wroclaw, 137, 140–1443; history, 140–142; museums, 142
Wyzynski, Stefan (Cardinal), 59

Zakopane, 84
Zamosc, 97
Zelazowa Wola, 64
Zobrowka, 67

TRAVEL THE WORLD WITH HIPPOCRENE BOOKS!

HIPPOCRENE INSIDER'S GUIDES:
The series which takes you beyond the tourist track to give you an insider's view:

NEPAL
PRAKASH A. RAJ
0091 ISBN 0-87052-026-1 $9.95 paper

HUNGARY
NICHOLAS T. PARSONS
0921 ISBN 0-87052-976-5 $16.95 paper

ROME
FRANCES D'EMILIO
0520 ISBN 0-87052-027-X $14.95 paper

MOSCOW, LENINGRAD AND KIEV (Revised)
YURI FEDOSYUK
0024 ISBN 0-87052-881-5 $11.95 paper

PARIS
ELAINE KLEIN
0012 ISBN 0-87052-876-9 $14.95 paper

POLAND (Third Revised Edition)
ALEXANDER T. JORDAN
0029 ISBN 0-87052-880-7 $9.95 paper

TAHITI (Revised)
VICKI POGGIOLI
0084 ISBN 0-87052-794-0 $9.95 paper

THE FRENCH ANTILLES (Revised)
ANDY GERALD GRAVETTE
The Caribbean islands of Guadeloupe, Martinique, St. Bartholomew, and St. Martin, and continental Guyane (French Guiana)
0085 ISBN 0-87052-105-5 $11.95 paper

THE NETHERLANDS ANTILLES: A TRAVELER'S GUIDE
The Caribbean islands of Aruba, Bonaire, Curacao, St. Maarten, St. Eustatius, and Saba.
0240 ISBN 0-87052-581-6 $9.95 paper

HIPPOCRENE LANGUAGE AND TRAVEL GUIDES:
Because traveling is twice as much fun if you can meet new people as well as new places!

MEXICO
ILA WARNER
An inside look at verbal and non-verbal communication, with suggestions for sightseeing on and off the beaten track.
0503 ISBN 0-87052-622-7 $14.95 paper

HIPPOCRENE COMPANION GUIDES:
Written by American professors for North Americans who wish to enrich their travel experience with an understanding of local history and culture.

SOUTHERN INDIA
JACK ADLER
Covers the peninsular states of Tamil Nadu, Andhra Pradesh, and Karnataka, and highlights Goa, a natural gateway to the south.
0632 ISBN 0-87052-030-X $14.95 paper

AUSTRALIA
GRAEME and TAMSIN NEWMAN
0671 ISBN 0-87052-034-2 $16.95 paper

IRELAND
HENRY WEISSER
0348 ISBN 0-87052-633-2 $14.95 paper

POLAND
JILL STEPHENSON and ALFRED BLOCH
"An appealing amalgam of practical information, historical curiosities, and romantic forays into Polish culture"--*Library Journal*
0894 ISBN 0-87052-636-7 $11.95 paper

PORTUGAL
T. J. KUBIAK
2305 ISBN 0-87052-739-8 $14.95 paper

ROMANIA
LYDLE BRINKLE
0351 ISBN 0-87052-634-0 $14.95 paper

THE SOVIET UNION
LYDLE BRINKLE
0357 ISBN 0-87052-635-9 $14.95 paper

THE CEMETERY BOOK
TOM WEIL
The ultimate guide to spirited travel describes burial grounds, catacombs, and similar travel haunts the world over (or under).
0106 ISBN 0-87052-916-1 $22.50 cloth

GUIDE TO EAST AFRICA:
KENYA, TANZANIA, AND THE SEYCHELLES (Revised)
NINA CASIMATI
0043 ISBN 0-87052-883-1 $14.95 paper

TRAVEL SAFETY:
SECURITY AND SAFEGUARDS AT HOME AND ABROAD
JACK ADLER and THOMAS C. TOMPKINS
0034 ISBN 0-87052-884-X $8.95 paper

And three books by GEORGE BLAGOWIDOW to keep you on your toes:

TRAVELER'S TRIVIA TEST:
1,101 QUESTIONS AND ANSWERS FOR THE SOPHSTICATED GLOBETROTTER
0087 ISBN 0-87052-915-3 $6.95 paper

TRAVELER'S I.Q. TEST:
RATE YOUR GLOBETROTTING KNOWLEDGE
0103 ISBN 0-87052-307-4 $6.95 paper

TRAVELER'S CHALLENGE:
SOPHISTICATED GLOBETROTTER'S RECORD BOOK
0398 ISBN 0-87052-248-5 $6.95 paper

TO PURCHASE HIPPOCRENE'S BOOKS contact your local bookstore, or write to Hippocrene Books, 171 Madison Avenue, New York, NY 10016. Please enclose a check or money order, adding $3 shipping (UPS) for the first book, and 50 cents for each of the others.
Write also for our full catalog of maps and foreign language dictionaries and phrasebooks.

GUIDE TO BLACK AMERICA
MARCELLA THUM
Historic homes, art and history museums, parks, monuments, landmarks of the civil rights movement, battlefields and forts, colleges and churches throughout the United States.
0722 ISBN 0-87052-045-8 $11.95 paper

THE GUIDE TO BLACK WASHINGTON:
PLACES AND EVENTS OF HISTORICAL AND CULTURAL SIGNIFICANCE IN THE NATION'S CAPITAL
SANDRA FITZPATRICK and MARIA GOODWIN
"Wonderful"--Kathryn Smith, President, Washington Historical Society
0025 ISBN 0-87052-832-7 $14.95 paper

WEST POINT AND THE HUDSON VALLEY
GALE KOHLHAGEN and ELLEN HEINBACH
Foreword by GENERAL DAVE R. PALMER, SUPERINTENDENT OF WEST POINT
An insider's guide to the stories, sites, cadet life and lore of the U.S. Military Academy; with side trips to great estates, historic sites, and wineries.
0083 ISBN 0-87052-889-0 $14.95 paper

UNCOMMON AND UNHERALDED MUSEUMS
BEVERLY NARKIEWICZ and LINCOLN S. BATES
500 regional and thematic museums across the nation.
0052 ISBN 0-87052-956-0 $14.95 paper

THE SOUTHWEST:
A FAMILY ADVENTURE
TISH MINEAR and JANET LIMON
An imaginative guide exploring the Colorado Plateau through Utah, Colorado, Arizona, and New Mexico.
0394 ISBN 0-87052-640-5 $16.95 paper

RV:
TRAVEL LEISURELY YEAR ROUND
ROLANDA DUMAIS MASSE
Practical, first-hand advice on living in a recreational vehicle with independence and economy.
0058 ISBN 0-87052-958-7 $14.95 paper

EXPLORING THE BERKSHIRES (Revised)
HERBERT S. WHITMAN
Illustrated by ROSEMARY FOX
"A gem of a book"--Conde Nast's *Traveler*
0925 ISBN 0-87052-979-X $9.95 paper

By the same authors:
EXPLORING NANTUCKET
"Anyone contemplating a visit to this island would benefit from this book"--
Library Journal
0046 ISBN 0-87052-792-4 $11.95 paper

LONG ISLAND:
A GUIDE TO NEW YORK'S SUFFOLK AND NASSAU COUNTIES (Revised)
RAYMOND, JUDITH and KATHRYN SPINZIA
0088 ISBN 0-87052-879-3 $17.50 paper

TO PURCHASE HIPPOCRENE'S BOOKS contact your local bookstore, or write to
Hippocrene Books, 171 Madison Avenue, New York, NY 10016. Please enclose a
check or money order, adding $3 shipping (UPS) for the first book, and 50 cents for
each of the others.